The King of Gravesend

a pack of lies

from

Peter Draper

Chapter 1

Riding the golf cart through the walkways at Heathrow Airport's Terminal 5, the Purser from American Airlines flight AA56 clutched the sealed manilla envelope close to his chest and flashed the occasional glance at his companion. The airport driver skilfully swerved around the passengers who were slowly walking towards immigration and eventually arrived at the lone counter set off to one side.

"Here we are, Sir," the Purser said, "Let's get you sorted out shall we? I think you may have to be debriefed by your immigration people and there will be some serious repercussions for your actions in the United States, but I do wish you well."

They both walked towards the counter, staffed by a lone immigration officer, and the purser handed over the envelope. The Officer gave a curt "Thanks," took the envelope and said, "Deportation?"

"Correct," the Purser replied with a flourish, only to be ignored by the immigration officer who never once looked him in the eye, and simply reached under the counter and pressed a button to summon the Airport Police.

The purser stood there awkwardly until the officer gave him a dismissive "you can go now" look. He stayed there for just long enough for it to get really uncomfortable before giving up and going back to the golf cart, which drove away without him just as he approached it.

The Immigration Officer smiled then said, "Won't keep you a minute, just waiting for my colleague."

A few minutes later a Police Woman walked over to the counter and took the envelope, she broke the seal and opened it, reaching inside for the passport and the bundle of paperwork. She checked the passport identity page against the man standing at the counter, then said," Mr. Douglas? Charles Douglas?"

"Yes Ma'am but they tend to call me Chuds."

"Yeah, I'm not gonna do that Mr. Douglas, deported were we?"

"Well I was, I can't speak for you," and he flashed her a cheeky smile to let her know he was joking.

She was obviously unimpressed with the quick display of wit, "Did they treat you okay?"

"About as well as I deserved. Honestly I've paid money to stay in worse places than the Buffalo Federal Detention Facility."

"Well, welcome home," and she handed the passport and the envelope over, turned and walked away.

"What she said," the Immigration Officer said and waved him through.

Chapter 2

Charlie "Chuds" Douglas had been out of the United Kingdom for 18 years, living and illegally working in various parts of the United States until finally they caught up with him. He had served a few months in Federal Detention that was designed to make you hate the US and never be tempted to return, before they sent him with two ICE Officers to Washington Dulles Airport. They stuck him on an American Airlines flight bound for Heathrow with a rice sack containing some of his clothes, his wallet and two hundred Canadian Dollars which was the money in his pocket when they arrested him.

Unsure of what to expect when he reached Heathrow, his entry into the country was, thankfully, relatively easy. He found a money changer and turned the Canadian money into Pounds and came away with about 100. Thinking that wouldn't last long he found an ATM, there had been a few dollars left in an American bank account before his arrest and thankfully that was still there, so he pulled a few more pounds out, and headed towards the Heathrow Express.

None of this had been here when he left the country, a ride to or from Heathrow was either with a family member or an expensive taxi, and looking at the two self ticketing machines Chuds became very confused. He walked around a little trying to find an employee and finally came across a manned ticket office, tucked away in the corner. The clerk was looking at his phone, not looking rather staring at his phone, and didn't even see Chuds at the counter.

"Excuse me"

"What?" didn't even look up.

"What's the cheapest way to get to Central London?"

"Walking I think Mate," still didn't look up.

Chuds waited a while, absorbing the sheer rudeness of someone that only had one job, to sell tickets on this train, and couldn't even be bothered to make eye contact. Eventually the clerk must have realized that his 'customer' was still at his window and decided to look up, "What?"

"Let's try this again, I've been out of the country for a while and have no idea what it costs to get to Central London on this train, so can you tell me what would be the cheapest way to get to there... Please."

"Fourteen quid mate, one way."

"There that wasn't so hard was it, I'll take one ticket please."

"It's a lot easier to use the machine," the clerk replied. You could see he was desperate to get back to his phone.

"Easier for you maybe, but I don't work for this railroad and you do, so can you sell me one ticket to a London Terminal and we can put this whole, unpleasant conversation behind us."

"For fuck's sake," the clerk muttered under his breath, but printed the ticket, took the money and gave Chuds his change.

"Thanks, you should probably take a nap now, after all that hard work."

"Fuck you," the clerk replied.

Chuds walked away, wondering if customer service in England was this bad everywhere.

Eventually he found the right platform and when the train arrived he settled into a seat by a window. As the train pulled away he looked at the scenery until his eyes closed. The movement of the train was relaxing and while not asleep he just let the journey pass until he sensed he was getting close to the city.

Opening his eyes, he looked out at the homes, and industrial parks until the train pulled into Paddington Station. Grabbing the sack, he got out onto the platform and walked through the barrier and out onto the street.

Ah, London. It had been almost twenty years since he had been in this city, a lot had changed it seemed, but there was always a certain consistency with the city. The old buildings kept London grounded in its past and allowed you to see past the tacky souvenir and grocery shops.

London had survived so much, in its history it had endured through fires, plagues, wars and more. The population was constantly changing with immigration and migration, and at street level the shops matched the needs of that glorious mix. However, if you simply looked up at the incredible architecture, it would always be London. The buildings told the story of the city, from the square mile of the City to the majesty of the parks and palaces, the archways, the back alleys of the East End, they all told a story of the city that can never be defeated. London wore its history like a badge of honour.

Did it feel good to be back?

Chuds thought about it and decided it really didn't, but here he was and he'd make the most of it.

Chapter 3

It was chilly, but dry, and to save money Chuds decided to walk to Charing Cross Station where he could get a train back to his home town. It would give him a chance to reminisce about the good old days, and even the not so good ones. It was a decent walk, probably about an hour or more, but really, what else did he have to do?

Walking by Hyde Park the flowers were beautiful. Bright yellow daffodils lined the fences and as he walked along Bayswater Road he saw the huge artworks, A giant horse's head seemingly defying gravity, a herd of bronze elephants and the magnificent Marble Arch marked the start of Oxford Street, and he carried on past the huge department stores and tried to see what shops he could remember.

Selfridges was still there, looking as grand as ever. Chuds thought back to visiting the store at Christmas as a child, with the incredible window displays. His parents took him there many times and every year he seemed to remember the window displays getting better and better. He wondered if they still did those.

John Lewis and a few other major stores still seemed to be around but there was a proliferation of gaudy souvenir shops all seeming to sell the same tat. There were new clothing retailers that he had never heard of and overpriced coffee shops with speciality sandwiches, but the people seemed to be the same. A glorious mix of nationalities, elbowing and swerving their way around each other, hurrying to destinations unknown.

After crossing Regent Street he took a right and headed down through Soho, one of his old stomping grounds. Damn, he had gotten into some mischief here back in the day. The strip clubs had all gone, the dummy entrance ways that sold you a "ticket" to a club down the street were gone too. There seemed to be a few brasses, with their doorbells and postcards taped just inside the front door, still operating but their numbers were severely depleted too. There was the occasional sex shop but mostly small, boutique restaurants, coffee shops and some designer boutiques.

Soho used to be so "shifty and tacky" now it was "niche".

Strolling steadily down Berwick Street he crossed the road and went into Walker's Court, it felt good to see a couple of massage parlours and a peep show. At least the area had retained a little of its old heritage as the smut centre of London. He was sad to see that the Raymond Revue Bar was gone though, he'd had a few adventures there. The old owner Paul Raymond, while not exactly a friend, had certainly been an acquaintance worth knowing.

Following the old roads that he had known so well Chuds went into Leicester Square, almost every venue that he had known, and sometimes managed, had gone. The London Experience and the small cinema and theatre club in Gerrard Street, all gone. Now in Leicester Square, a huge M&M theme shop dominated the corner.

"A theme shop for fucking sweets," Chuds muttered, and shook his head, but kept walking anyway. Charing Cross station was just a few minutes away and he just absorbed the nostalgia, went past Trafalgar Square and made his way to the grand exterior of the hotel and station. He sighed, and realized this was it, he was going home to a place he hadn't called home for almost two decades.

Walking through one of the archways the station didn't seem to have changed much. A lot of people and a few policemen, armed apparently, thronged the ticketing area, and Chuds looked at the self-ticketing machines with horror.

Does nobody work at these places any more, why do they expect paying customers to do the jobs of their clerks? This was not an improvement as far as Chuds was concerned and he walked around them and approached a ticketing window.

A cheerful looking lady asked how she could help, and Chuds asked for a single to Gravesend. The lady smiled broadly, tapped on a monitor and asked him for Thirteen Pounds and Seventy Pence please.

"No, a single please, just one way, to Gravesend."

"Been a while has it? Thirteen Seventy please darling, cash or card?"

Chuds pulled the American debit card from his pocket and placed it on the small turntable.

"Try that card, if it doesn't go through I'll pay cash."

The turntable revolved and the ever smiling lady took it and swiped it through a machine, "Let's have a go shall we?"
To his surprise it worked and he thanked her profusely and took the ticket.

"You should get a job at Heathrow Express darlin' there's a miserable bastard working there that could learn customer service from you."

"I'll look into that," she smiled, with a hint of sarcasm, and closed with, "Enjoy the ride."

There was about thirty minutes until the next train was due to leave so Chuds pulled a crumpled piece of paper from his wallet and looked at his daughter's phone number. There had been no contact with his kids for almost 5 months while the US Government had kept him in the detention facility and it seemed a good idea to call her and let her know he was okay, and ask if maybe he could stay with her until he got back on his feet.

Finding a payphone it seemed to only take cards, but he had no idea how to dial the number. He didn't know if he needed to add a prefix to the number, should he leave off the first 0? He decided to ask and walked over to a transport cop, explained his situation and problem to the seemingly disinterested officer, who looked at him with complete disdain.

"Do I look like fucking directory enquiries?" and he turned away.

A ready retort came to mind, but having just spent almost five months in an American Detention Facility, he decided that discretion was the better part of valour and walked over to the platform. The train had just pulled in and he climbed onboard and found a window seat.

Not normally the nervous type, Chuds felt a small amount of anxiety creep into his mind and, as the train pulled slowly away, he stared out of the window.

He watched as central London changed to suburban London and eventually gave way to Kent. Much of the scenery was familiar but a lot was not. Taking it all in he waited until the train pulled up at Gravesend and got off. Leaving the platform and passing the ticket barrier he stepped out into the sunshine and took a deep breath.

"This should be interesting."

Chapter 4

Breathing in the air and holding his face towards the sun, a lot of memories came flooding back. Looking to his left there was a taxi rank, to his right he could walk up towards the town centre. With only limited funds he decided against the taxi and walked towards the town. He needed to find a familiar face, but after all this time would any of them still be familiar?

Back in the day, one of his best friends had been Ronnie Atwood, commonly known as "Wrong Way Ronnie" and if Chuds wanted to place a bet on where to find him it would be in one of two pubs. So holding his battered sack tight he walked up and crossed over into Windmill Street and turned left towards the Borough Shades, except when he got there it wasn't there any more.

The Borough, as it used to be known, had been a unique pub, you entered a small delicatessen first then brushed through a bead curtain into a long bar. As pubs went it was pretty classy, unlike some of the clientele, and had a real fireplace, comfortable seating and a long and well stocked bar. It had been one of their favourite haunts for lunchtime and evening drinks and 'pub grub', now it was a failed retro bar, all boarded up.

Plan B, carry on down to The King's Head, right next door to the old ABC Cinema that Chuds had managed once upon a time. The pub was still there but now was advertising itself as a sports bar, still it was open and Ronnie might be there, and maybe he could get a lift to his daughter's house.

Surprise number one was that there was a bouncer at the door, no ID needed and apparently Chuds didn't look like a threat, "times change," he muttered. He walked into the lounge and while it was essentially the same place it had lost the 'Pub Feel', now fairly sterile with the few customers staring at wall mounted TV screens but there in the corner, alone at a table, was Ronnie. He had a full pint of beer in front of him so Chuds bought his own from the bar and walked over to the table. He stood at the table waiting for Ronnie to notice him, it took a while, he was staring at a phone screen, probably checking on bets that he had placed, but eventually he looked up. It took a few seconds for him to recognize his old friend, but then his jaw dropped and he smiled broadly.

"Fuck me runnin'! Chuds! Where you been? It was your round about 20 fuckin' years ago, I'll 'ave a pint."

"You've already got a pint Ronnie, I'll fill it for you later, how you been?"

"Oh mustn't grumble Chuds, could be worse, 'ave a seat and tell me everything you know, I've got a couple of minutes spare."

The two men sipped their beers and Chuds caught Ronnie up on his current situation.

Ronnie, to no surprise, was still single, still gambling, still drinking and still "earnin' a livin' wiv a bit of this and a bit of that and none of the other".

He had earned the nickname "Wrong Way Ronnie" because if there was a choice to be made in any situation, he would undoubtedly choose the wrong one. From deciding whether to turn left or right while driving to "taking a punt" on a business venture, the smart money was to choose the opposite of what Ronnie suggested. He probably still had a shed full of Betamax video recorders because he just knew they would win the format wars.

However his major skill, and one in which he excelled, was knowing the right man for the right job, he could fix things for you. You needed a job? Ronnie knew a man. Need a place to stay? Ronnie's brother's, cousin's, aunt had a spare room. It felt good to be back talking to his old friend.

After finishing their beers, Chuds walked over to the bar and had the glasses filled, a pint of bitter for Ronnie and a draught Guinness for himself. Nobody in the bar, apart from Ronnie, had a clue who he was.

Taking a sip from his glass, Ronnie looked at his old friend and asked, "So, Chuds, noticed anything different about the old place?"

"Which place Ronnie, the boozer or the town?"

"Well both, but the town mostly."

"The boozer feels strange, because you're the only face I know. There was a time I couldn't walk in here without almost everyone knowing me."

"Well, you did manage the old cinema next door, right?

"Yeah back in 1974. Blazing Saddles was playing when I took the job as Assistant Manager, I knew every line from that movie, back then. What happened to it?"

"Well, Bluewater opened a big and posh multi-screen Chuds. It killed the local place. Then a group of Indians bought it out to show Bollywood films, but even they couldn't make it pay. Finally there was a fire and now it's just all boarded up. Cryin' shame if you ask me."

"What's a Bluewater?"

"Big Mall, Chuds, in Greenhithe, I'll take you there whenever you want to go."

"That can wait Ronnie, any chance you could run me out to my daughter's place?"

"Of course there is Chuds, finish your beer, we'll go now."

Chapter 5

"What's a Ka?" Chuds asked as they walked to the car park.

"It's a car innit? A Ford car to be exact."

"Bit small isn't it Ronnie?"

" 'ave you seen the price of petrol Chuds? Fill the tank it's like being mugged, this is a compact innit. Economical as they say."

Chuds got into the front passenger seat and Ronnie started the Ka car and they set off. He pulled away in second gear and the car stuttered until it found its groove and they set of for the outskirts of town.

Ronnie stayed in second, the engine and gears were whining, then screaming, for a gear change.

"Wanna change gears Ronnie? Try putting in third."

"Sorry Chuds," the engine gave a sigh of relief as he took it out of second right up until he crashed it straight into fourth gear. The car juddered but eventually got its rhythm again and somehow kept on rolling.

Checking out the top of the gear stick Chuds saw that this was a five speed, so he ventured, "Why not put it into fifth Ronnie?"

"Is there one?"

"Who the fuck taught you to drive Ronnie, I mean I'm grateful for the lift but really you're killing this car."

"It was TGT Chuds. Two Gear Tony, he said I'm a natural."

"At what? 'Cause it sure ain't at driving Ronnie."

"Wanna walk instead Chuds?"

"No, we're good, but don't ask me to push when you kill the gearbox."

Once they reached his daughter's house Chuds offered Ronnie some petrol money for the ride.

"No need Chuds, good to see you back."

"I'd like to say it's good to BE back Ronnie, but the jury's still out on that."

Ronnie scribbled his mobile number on the back of a petrol receipt and gave it to his friend.

"Call me if you need anything."

"Sure thing, and thanks again Ronnie."

Chapter 6

His daughter was both surprised and relieved to see her Dad. The US Government did not allow international phone calls from the detention facility and it was not until he had been allocated a public defender that he had been able to get word out that he was okay, just 'unavoidably detained'.

"Ever thought of calling to let me know you were coming Dad?"

"I tried from Charing Cross, but at the risk of sounding like a doddery old bastard I couldn't work out how to use the new-fangled phones."

"Sounds about right, ya doddery old bastard," and she hugged him hard and long.

Then the grand kids turned up and joined in and somehow there must have been dust in the room because Chuds' eyes started to water.

"Any chance I can stay here for a few days until I decompress and sort myself out?"

"Of course, stay as long as you like Dad."

He definitely felt like he needed a couple of days to sort his head out, find a way to make some money and somewhere to live that was closer to the town. First, though, some family bonding. It had been a long time since he'd seen his family. Even though he had only been detained for just under 5 months, it brought home how precious it is to be able to walk free, reconnect with family, meet old friends and not be told what to do at all times.

Once his son and family came over the reunion was complete. Tears wanted to flow, but Chuds held them back as much as he could. The grand kids made fun of the faces he was pulling trying not to cry and were just happy to play with him. Many stories were swapped, everyone was keen to know the deportation story and Chuds was happy to tell it, with only minor embellishments.

However, a plan needed to be formed. Income needed to be arranged and he needed a place to stay that was within walking distance of the town centre. There was no doubt in his mind that Ronnie could help with all of these things, there were bound to be rooms available and someone would surely be hiring.

Chuds had found throughout his life that if you had a job you could always get another. That first step was always the hardest, being unemployed it was often so difficult to get a foot on the first rung of the employment ladder. He called Ronnie and asked for a ride into the town, whenever he had a spare moment.

"Let me check my schedule Chuds.. 'ang on.. move that.. change that.. looks like I've got a free spot.. now. I'll be there in about 20 minutes."

"Top man Ronnie, I'll be waiting outside for you."

Putting on some clean clothes then hugging on the grand kids for a while, Chuds took his time. There was no way Ronnie would be there in 20 minutes, but he was ready in time anyway and stepped outside into the fresh Kent air. It was not cold, but there was a strong breeze that carried a chill factor and the sun shone brightly. He took in some deep breaths of air and relished the feeling.

If only it could stay like this, but a living needed to be earned and a plan of action allowed to develop.

Listening intently, head turned against the wind, he heard the unmistakable whining of Ronnie's Ka, as the gearbox screamed to be released, eventually a crunching sound and the lower tone of fourth gear. Ronnie had slammed it into fourth just in time to slow down to take the corner at the end of the street. The car juddered, tried to stall but was no match for Ronnie's mastery of the pedals, then eventually pulled up to a halt outside of the house. Putting it into neutral, Ronnie wound down the window.

"Mornin' Chuds! "Ow's yer belly off for spots? C'mon get in, I ain't got all day."

"Oh, schedule packed is it Ronnie? Well, I appreciate you taking time out of your day for me."

"Anytime Chuds, now get in, I'm wasting petrol here."

Climbing into the front seat, Chuds put the seat belt on. His last trip with Ronnie had been traumatic enough for him to make sure he took every precaution available. Putting the car into second Ronnie played with the accelerator and clutch pedals and the car shuddered away trying desperately to stall.

Taking a deep breath Chuds closed his eyes and thought that if he was a religious sort he'd be praying about now. Once they were on the main road, and Ronnie had slammed the tortured gearbox into fourth, the car settled in and Chuds asked his friend if he knew of anyone hiring.

"What you lookin' for Chuds? What type of work?"

"Anything really Ronnie, just need to put some cash in the old sky rocket and you know, when you have a job it's always easier to get a job."

"I hear ya Chuds. Lemme think a bit."

Chuds tried hard to relax but Ronnie's driving was doing everything it could to prevent that from happening. He looked over at him and asked, "So what's happening in the old town Ronnie?"

"It's gone downhill a bit to be honest Chuds. There's been a lot of newcomers from Eastern Europe, Serbs, Kosovans, bit of Liquorish Allsorts really. They brought some crime with 'em, different crime. 'Arder drugs, lots of prossies, some long con games and scavenging."

"Scavenging?"

"Yeah they send the kids out to go through the bin bags outside of people's 'ouses. They look for bank statements, credit card bills, any kind of bill really. Then they use them to hack people's accounts or steal their identity to buy lots of shit online. The Old Bill can't do much about it to be honest, once the bags are outside they're fair game. Your only protection is to shred any paperwork, or better still, burn it in the back garden."

"They organized Ronnie? They got a main man?"

"Really don't know Chuds, I stay clear, I just do my bits and pieces, make a bob or two 'ere and there, when I can."

After a few minutes of silence, except of the sound of the poor gear box praying for fifth, Ronnie coughed then with a sideways glance at Chuds, which made him even more nervous, asked for some advice.

"Hey, maybe you can help me. My niece has a birthday comin' up. She's gonna be eleven, any idea what I can get her for a pressie?"

"How about a nice book Ronnie?"

"Oh she's already got a book Chuds."

Chuds sighed and waited for the ride to end.

Chapter 7

Ronnie pulled the car into what used to be an outdoor market but was now a Borough car park. He did something on his phone, then said, "All set. Parkin' paid for, let's go see a man about a dog."

"That's it? Twiddle with your phone and you've paid for the car parking?"

"Yep! Smart phones Chuds, they're a thing of beauty."

"Probably smarter than I feel right now Ronnie. I'll have to get one of those as soon as I can get some work."

"Well, I think I can help you there. My sister's married to an Eyetie, decent enough geezer Chuds, he's got a restaurant in the High Street, maybe he can help you out. Let's go see him."

Ronnie locked the car and the two men walked through a small alleyway into the High Street, they turned right and they were facing the town pier and the River Thames. The Thames had provided employment for Chud's family for generations.

His late Granddad had been a lighterman and bargeman on the river up until he retired. His Uncle had worked on the docks and they had both apprenticed with his great grandfather, whom he had never met. Chud's dad had been tipped to follow in their footsteps, but it turned out there wasn't much call for river workers that got seasick on the Gravesend to Tilbury ferry, so he had become an electrician instead.

"I love that River," Chuds said, almost under his breath.

Just a short way down the road they came to an Italian restaurant, "Giovanni's Family Restaurant", to be precise. Ronnie pushed open the door and they both entered.

"Chuds, this is my brother in law."

The owner put his hand out and as Chuds shook it he said, "Giovanni I presume?"

"No, I'm Steve. But there's not a lot of call for an Italian Restaurant called "Steve's" so we picked that name just for the sign."

Steve's smile was broad and his handshake strong and hearty.

"I heard a fair bit about you Chuds. Sorry to hear about you getting thrown out of the States."

"Well, you know, shit happens Steve. So Ronnie said you might have a job going?"

"We can always use a dishwasher Chuds. As long as you don't think that's too menial, I mean Ronnie told me you ran this town at one time."

Ronnie cut in "Oh yeah, he was the King of..."

"Not now Ronnie," Chuds cut him off firmly, "Yeah I used to have my fingers in a few pies, but things change. I'll take whatever's going, to be honest, and I promise you'll get 100% effort if you give me a start."

" Well, we sell a few pies here and the plates all need to be cleaned so, fair enough, you're hired, when can you start?"

"Is now too soon?"

"Well, let's say tomorrow, be here at 4:00 pm we'll get you started."

"Steve I truly appreciate this, I won't let you down."

As they left the restaurant Chuds thanked Ronnie for the introduction.

"Really appreciate that Ronnie, you did me a solid there, I won't forget it."

"No problem Chuds, fancy a pint?

"Sure."

As they walked up the sloping High Street, Chuds noticed that many of the old pubs had changed and many shops that had served the town for generations had gone. He wasn't against change but always hoped that it was in the name of progress, That didn't seem to the case here. It was, however, nice to see a couple of independent cafes and coffee shops, and he suggested that they pop into one for a snack and a coffee.

"Coffee? You turned right Yank over there didn't you? I'll have a cuppa if that's okay. You buyin' ?"

"Sure, I mean I'm employed now and everything right? My treat Ronnie."

They walked into the small cafe, looked around and picked the table by the window. Chuds wanted to see the people walking by and get a feel for the town again. He ordered a cup of tea and a black coffee and asked if they had any scones.

The woman behind the counter was about twenty five years old, tattooed and had really big holes in her earlobes that were filled with a hollow ring. He found out later that they were called "flesh tunnels" which seemed apt, but for now he couldn't stop staring at them.

"Got an eyeful, have ya?"

Chuds apologized for staring and told the girl that he had been out of the country for a while, he nodded towards her ears and complimented her, "Never seen piercings like that before, they look, err... nice. So, do you have scones?"

"Scones? What do you think this is, an old Lyons Corner House? We got muffins, cookies and a couple of bits of banana bread. All home made, not at my home though," and she giggled at her own joke.

"We'll take the banana bread, thanks," and he gave her a five pound note as payment.

"You're gonna need a bit more than that. You have been away for a while, haven't you?"

He gave her the extra cash and walked back to the window seat. She brought the drinks and snacks over when they were ready and Chuds thanked her and said, "Sorry about staring at your ears before, I think they look good. By the way, how do you know what a Lyons Corner House was?"

"My old granny used to work in one, up in the smoke, I seen the pictures, black and white of course."
Chuds mentally aged about twenty years hearing her speak, she turned, walked back behind the counter and started looking at her phone again. He looked at Ronnie who was doing exactly the same thing.

Staring at phone screens seemed to be the new national obsession, maybe he wouldn't get one too soon. He had business to take care of.

Ronnie added three heaped teaspoons of sugar to his milky tea, stirred it and then took a sip.

"Lovely cuppa Chuds, cheers."

"You're welcome Ronnie, the town has changed quite a bit eh?"

"More than I like Chuds, and not so much for the better if you ask me."

"Yeah, I'm noticing that."

They drank their beverages, ate their banana bread and Chuds continued to watch the passers-bye as they walked up and down the street.

"Hey Ron, does 'Two-Loos Terry' still own that pub in Northfleet? The Red Lion?"

"Sure does Chuds, he's doin' pretty good too. One of the few boozers still putting on live music and he's changed the place a bit and this time for the better."

"Man, we had some good times down there, didn't we?"

"Yeah, remember that night you and Andy went all punk?"

Chapter 8

October 20th 1980 – The night of the world's shortest lived punk band.

Chuds and Andy were sitting at the bar of the Red Lion. It was a Tuesday and Tuesday's were affectionately called "Spiky Night" after the punk rock hair styles of the kids that came every week to hear the latest punk and ska bands play.

Early Spiky Night drinks were a fairly common occurrence for them as, before the crowd started to arrive, it was always quiet and it was possible to chat with Terry. Once the punters started to arrive though, the suspicious looks started flying at "the old guys" at the bar, the noise level ramped up and when the three chord wonders started playing it became impossible to talk. That's when they usually went home. Not this evening though.

While Andy and Chuds sat at the bar chatting, Terry the Landlord, was getting the bar ready, wiping down the counters, checking the beer pumps and making sure there were snacks ready for sale. Then the door opened and one of the biggest human beings they had ever seen walked into the bar. He had a shaved head, was dressed in a Ben Sherman shirt, Jeans and Doc Martin boots and he walked towards the bar.

Terry looked up briefly and said, "Fuck off. I don't serve skinheads, never have and never will."

The enormous man simply said. "Fair enough," turned and left.

That was the last time any of them saw him until he appeared as the lead singer of a rising ska band on the next week's Top of The Pops television show.

That evening, though, nobody thought much of the incident until, as the time went by, Terry realized that the band hadn't shown up to set up and sound check. He grabbed the phone and called the booker who informed him that as Terry had just told the band's singer to fuck off, they were actually driving home while they spoke.

"You're still paying the fee though, they did their part and turned up."

Terry's head dropped forward and he sighed deeply.

"What am I gonna do guys? That was the band I just told to get lost. In about an hour I'll have over a hundred drinking age kids in here and no music for them. I'm screwed."

Andy and Chuds sipped their beers, then looked at each other and Andy said, "Never fear Tel. We'll do it."

Chuds had played bass guitar in a few bands that Andy had fronted, he hadn't played it well and, if truth be told, he had mostly stood in until Andy found a real bass player. Currently he was helping out in Andy's band, suspiciously called "Slippery Biscuit" playing mostly progressive rock, some older rock covers and a few original numbers.

The Lion had a back line of amps and speakers in place and a ready to go PA System. All they would need was a drum kit and their guitars. Chuds thought briefly and said, "Let's call Wrong Way Ronnie to get the others, Tom's drums and our guitars. We can do this. Terry can I use your blower?"

So the calls were made. Tom would get ready and load his kit up in Ronnie's van, then they would pick up Andy's girlfriend, Mark the singer, the two guitars and head over to the Red Lion. The whole process took about an hour and while they waited the punky punters started to drift in. Terry played some Pistols and Buzzcocks over the PA, but as the crowd grew so did the questions about who was going to be playing.

Eventually the van arrived and they quickly started to set up. The look of distrust in the customer's faces was evident as what appeared, to them, to be a bunch of old guys started setting up the drums and tuning up.

Andy's girlfriend, Annie and Tom's wife, Sandy had come along and Sandy had brought their young baby. Terry settled them behind the bar, the baby wearing ear muffs to protect his ears.

"One.. One..Two.. Check" The mic was working, the guitars were in tune(ish) and the band huddled around the singer to discuss what to play.

"Let's bang out a twelve bar, anything Status Quo like, but Tom, double the tempo. Let's go."

They did, Tom hit the sticks together 4 times and started to lay down a ferocious tempo. Andy looked at Chuds, nodded and mouthed the words, "Two.. Three.. Go."

Chords crashed in, the bass line picked up and, to be honest, it sounded pretty good. After a few bars they looked at Mark and suddenly realized, not only did he not know the words to the song, there actually were no words to the song. He shrugged, grabbed the mic and started to yell out the signs around the pub.

"Quarter pound burgers only a quid. Special offer on real ale. Gents toilets this way. Shepherd and Neame beers at best prices. Crisps, nuts and pork scratchings for sale."

If there was a notice or sign on the wall, or above the bar, Mark screamed it into the mic, and when he'd finished them all, he started again. After about 4 minutes Tom rolled a drum fill and crashed the song to a halt.

It went very quiet, then after a few uncomfortable seconds of silence they heard, "Fuck YEAH!"

"I hope you liked that 'cause we're doin' it again, three four," and they did.

As Chuds looked out at the crowd he could see that they had started pogoing, basically dancing by just jumping up and down in time with the song. Beer was flying from glasses and spraying the floor, which Terry loved because it meant they would buy more beer, more quickly. There were collisions between bouncing punks and fists pumping the air.

When the song finished for the second time the crowd cheered, Andy looked at the others and said, "You really Got Me" but double time, GO!

While they thrashed out the old Kinks classic at supersonic speed, Sandy started to change the baby's diaper. Just as the song finished she yelled loudly to Annie, at a volume designed to be heard over the music, "Ugh, he's done big runny number 2s," but the music had stopped and everyone heard.

Picking that as his cue, Mark yelled over the mic, "Good Evenin' Red Lion. We are The Big Runny Number Twos. We got another tune for ya now, but I need my back up singers."

Sandy and Annie jumped up on the stage, undid a couple of buttons on their blouses and stood behind Mark. As they thrashed their way through another song Mark was singing "Candy's Dandy, Ice is Nice but you can't get it on without the fluffy dice."

Ronnie ran to his van and grabbed his set of fluffy dice from the rear view mirror. Rushing back into the pub he threw them at Annie who immediately put them on as earrings. The girls moved up beside Mark and started to Doo-Wop and join in the chorus. At the end of the song they went back behind the bar, the crowd gave them a huge cheer and The Big Runny Number Twos played yet another song.

They played almost their entire repertoire of cover songs at double or triple tempo and Terry's eyes were beaming as the cash register cha-chinged away. Finally Terry flashed the light on the rear wall of the pub, signalling that the band should play the last song, and they finished with the same mess they had started the evening with.

"Thank you and good night!"

The crowd cheered and finished their beers, while the band joined Terry and the girls behind the bar. When the last spiky haircut had left the bar Terry beamed at the band.

"That was awesome guys, want me to book you in for next month?"

The band looked at each other, their shirts sticking to their bodies with sweat, hair wet, tired from all the jumping up and down and shook their heads.

"Not fuckin' likely Tel. That's too much like hard work."

Chapter 9

"Yeah, that was a great evening. The birth and death of The Big Runny Number Twos, one gig, no wages, formed and broke up the same night."

Finishing their beverages and snacks they got up from the table and as they walked over to the door Chuds looked back at the girl and said a cheery thanks and goodbye.

Without looking up from her phone she said, in a monotone, "What fucking ever."

"Charming," said Chuds as he stepped out into the High Street once again.

The two men continued walking up the High Street and crossed over into Windmill Street. This had been one of the streets that was the heart of the town when he had lived here before. Now two of the pubs were shuttered one of the huge shops was a national chain pub that looked more like a restaurant to Chuds' eyes. They carried on walking and just behind the Civic Center was one of his old haunts, The Prince Albert.

"Let's try here Ronnie," Chuds suggested and they entered through the doors.

Chuds looked around, and decided nothing had changed except the staff. He glanced over at the corner and there was one of his old crew, Brian Caldwell. Like almost everyone else nowadays he was staring at a phone screen and hadn't noticed Ronnie and Chuds enter the pub. There was a time when Brian would be on alert all the time, and knew who came in and out of every room he was in, those days seemed to have gone.

They walked over to the corner table and Chuds said, simply, "Brian."

He slowly raised his head, said, "Hey Chuds," and looked back to his phone. Then after a few seconds, like it was attached to a rubber sling shot, his head shot up and his jaw dropped.

"Chuds! When did you get back? How the fuck are you?"

"Just a few days ago Bri, mind if we sit?"

Brian nodded and as Chuds pulled over two stools Ronnie went to the bar and got three drinks in. Sitting at the table they all took a long sip of their drinks before Chuds started the conversation.

"So, Brian, how have you been? It's been a while eh?"

"Well, I guess I shouldn't grumble Chuds, but I probably will. I've not been good really, I've got that Post Dramatic Stress Disorder ain't I."

"Don't you mean Post Traumatic Brian?"

"Nope, it's Dramatic Chuds. Little things set me off, I can't stand fireworks now. Fucking Diwali around here almost kills me."

"What the hell happened to you Brian? What caused this condition?"

Brian took a long pull of his beer and leant back into the padding of the seat.

"Not really sure Chuds, but it keeps me on the disabled register and I get full benefits. Can't keep a job see. Nobody wants to hire someone who might kick off any minute."

"So, what you're saying is you've got a bad temper and you're skiving."

"Careful Chuds, you don't want me going off in 'ere do you?"
"Settle down Bri, let's have a chat. So what's going on?"

"I'll tell you my story if you tell me yours, Chuds. Where the hell 'ave you been for the last 20 years or so?"

Chuds filled him on on the deportation story and how he had spent the last 18 years. Nothing seemed to surprise Brian, who asked a couple of questions but mainly listened. In between sips of their beers the conversation flowed and Ronnie chimed in a couple of times too. Just three old friends catching up, but in truth, Brian didn't seem "right" to

Chuds. Not like the old mate who had got into a lot of mischief with him back in the day, more of a lonely guy who seemed frightened of the new world he found himself in.

"So, Bri, what's really bothering you?"

"I dunno Chuds. Nothing's the same as it was. All these Easterners here screwin' up the town. So much crime now."

"Brian, I hate to remind you but we did some crime here too."

"Not like this Chuds. Not hard drugs, not underage girls, we sold a bit of gear here and there, helped a few people out in the process, ran a few bets for a while. Mostly we 'ad a good time, and nobody got hurt, mostly nobody anyway. The Kosovan gits are different."

'You're coming off as a bit racist here Brian. This town has a long history of foreigners moving in and they've all settled into the town nicely as far as I remember. The Indians came, and they became a part of the community in record time. We started to call them GravesIndians if I remember right."

"Chuds, they came and integrated, they started businesses, opened shops, taxi firms, employed locals. They're good sorts, these are different."

"I dunno Brian, you just seem depressed to me. Like you're looking for something to justify you feeling down."

"I ain't just feeling down Chuds, I've got me Post Dramatic ain't I? I'm proper disabled now."

"Brian for the love of God it's post TRAUMATIC, and you have to have experienced TRAUMA to get the condition. What have you ever experienced that was traumatic, except that time that you woke up naked in bed with Fat Mona and Poncy Pete after that party at the Police Station?"

Chapter 10

February 14th 1983 – Brian's Valentine's Day Massacre

As part of its community outreach program the local Police Station was holding a Valentine's Day Dance in one of their large meeting rooms. This was an attempt to let prominent members of the community meet, mingle and hopefully find ways to all get along.

Chuds arrived that night with a gorgeous girl on his arm, wearing an expensive suit and a Crombie coat. His date was the second place winner of last year's Miss Gravesend competition, Sally Long, a blonde haired beauty with enormous breasts and a way of just looking good everywhere she went.

They made quite the couple, and Chuds, with his easy going manner and magnetic personality had no trouble walking around the crowd and either catching up with people he hadn't seen in a while or introducing himself to those he didn't know. Truthfully there were not many of those. He knew almost everyone of note and notoriety in the town.

Sally sipped from her Babycham and just clung to his arm.

Up on the small stage was the Police house band, "Red Amber and the Green Lights". They were all coppers, and played a nice mix of ballads and swing songs. A lot of couples were dancing and shuffling around the floor and in the back of the room was a makeshift bar selling beer and spirits that was attracting a few unsavoury characters. Chuds thought that quite a few of them should be in the cells in the building's basement, instead of in this room, but quite a few people thought the same about him probably.

His old friend Marvin was the singer of the band and was sitting on a high stool, holding the mic and crooning the lyrics. Not the right lyrics, but something close.

"Fly me to the moon and we can play amongst the cars..."

From the bass player behind him in a loud whisper, "Stars.. It's play amongst the fucking stars you prat."

Without a care in the world about the bass player's opinion, Marvin kept butchering the lyrics, but did it in a soulful baritone voice that seemed to let him get away with it. At an appropriate break in the song he spotted his old friend and said softly into the mic, "Chuds, good to see you."

Chuds nodded in return and Sally gave a slight wave, which she achieved without spilling a drop of her drink.

Continuing their walk around the room they came to the table where Wrong Way Ronnie and Brian were sitting. Brian was, at that time, the manager of a Bingo Hall and was there with his girlfriend, Brenda. Ronnie had a girl with him that Chuds didn't recognize and also at the table were Fat Mona and Poncy Pete. They were an unlikely couple, Mona was a "working girl" who specialized in customers that she affectionately called her "Chubby Chasers" and Poncy Pete managed a gay pub near the riverfront.

Chuds pulled a chair out and motioned for Sally to sit, which she did very elegantly. It was like she was always modelling instead of relaxing.

" 'Ave a seat Sal, carrying those tits around must be murder on your back," Ronnie said with a grin.

"Classy Ron, real classy," and Chuds shot him a disapproving look.

Sally seemed not to care, once sat she adjusted the top of her dress to avoid any kind of a wardrobe malfunction and returned to sipping her Babycham. Chuds noticed that no matter how many times she sipped at her drink, the glass never seemed to get any emptier. Some kind of Paul Daniels magic trick was going on there for sure, but it did make her a cheap date.

The Police often reached out to people like Pete so that they could trust them enough to report any wrong doings in their establishments. They never did though but Pete's pub was mainly full of gay men looking for company, a few local brasses drinking somewhere they felt safe and the occasional dodgy deal going down at a table. Still Pete was happy to be there, better to have the cops on your side than have them ignore you if you really had an emergency, and he was delighted to be there with Fat Mona. Everyone at the table looked to be having a good time and Ronnie ran over to get two chairs in case anyone else joined them.

Placing their drinks on the table the conversations started to flow and interweave. The girls swapped stories of their jobs and families, Fat Mona had them all roaring with laughter at some of her customer stories and Brian was telling of the near riot at the Bingo Hall when three customers all called "house" at the same time but didn't want to split their winnings.

"Mona?" Ronnie looked at the girl as she was chugging a light ale from the bottle, "When you work for Poncy as a barmaid I've seen you slam so many shots a sailor would be sick, yet you never seem to get drunk. " 'Ow do you do that?"

On days that Mona didn't want to work her usual job she often subbed in as a barmaid for Pete. On those nights the take was always high and the atmosphere was always electric. Mona accepted every offer of a drink from the customers and with her quick wit, suggestive jokes and outright flattery she easily doubled the take. Just as Ronnie had said, she drank so much alcohol but never got drunk.

Taking another long chug from her beer she looked at Ronnie and smiled.

"Well Ronnie, two things come to mind. First, unlike you, I can hold my drink like a real man not like a little girl like you. Secondly matey, I don't actually drink the shots. You know the beer bottle I keep behind the bar and how I always do a shot with a beer chaser?"

Ronnie nodded, and ignored the "little girl" dis.

"What I do is slam the shot into my mouth and keep it there, then I put the bottle in my mouth and spit it back into it. What looks like me doing a shot and chasin' it with a beer is me spitting the shot into the half empty bottle and later I pour it away in the sink."

"That's fucking alcohol abuse right there," Ronnie grumbled.

"Ask Pete if he minds me doin' that when he counts the money at the end of the night."

She looked over at Pete, who raised his glass to her and smiled broadly.

As the band had a break, Marvin walked over and putting one of his huge hands on Chud's shoulder said firmly, "You're fucking nicked mate."

"It's a fair cop Officer, I'll come quietly," Chuds said without even looking up.

"Like that would happen, so how are you Chuds? Fuck this table has some villains at it."

Chuds motioned for Marvin to join them at the table, but he declined, "Gotta mingle Chuds, Bosses orders."

"Not as many villains here as over there by the bar Marv. That sausage fest has some real badduns, you'd do better nickin' them all than wasting time with us honest business men."

"Honest business men? Is that what you're calling yourselves now?"

"Right up until you can prove different Marvin."

Squeezing Chud's shoulder Marvin wished them a good evening, told them all to stay out of trouble and wandered off to find more people to treat to his "You're nicked" routine.

Table by table the conversations got louder as the alcohol intake increased. The group at the bar looked like it was getting a little rowdy and eventually the band went back to destroying some classic songs.

Ronnie looked at Brian and said he thought it might all kick off at the bar, but Brian insisted nobody was going to be stupid enough to start a fight at a Police Station.

He was wrong.

In a very short space of time the voices of the men at the bar got louder and louder and the noise was only overcome by the sound of breaking glass as two men smashed bottles against the cinder block walls and squared off against each other. There was the requisite shouting, one or two people reluctantly trying to stop the fight breaking out and the crashing of cymbals as the band left the stage to rush to the scene of the fight.

"Seems like a good time to call it a night," Chuds suggested and the whole group rose from the table.

"Let's go to the boozer," Poncy Pete suggested, "We'll have a lock in."

Everyone agreed, except Brenda, who said she had a headache and was going home, but she told Brian to go ahead and enjoy himself, just not too much. The group grabbed their belongings, Sally reluctantly set her glass down on the table, and they all left the station as quickly as they could to walk to the riverfront.

There the party continued, after another hour or so Chuds took Sally home and dropped Ronnie and his date off along the way. Only Brian stayed at the pub for "just a couple more."

Brian, Mona and Pete kept the party going and soon were singing along to the juke-box and dancing and drinking. Eventually Brian had enough, he sat on one of the bench seats and gently fell forward, it was impossible to keep his eyes open, and he drifted into the unconscious sleep of the truly drunk.

When Mona and Pete had enough too she asked if it was okay to stay at the pub and Pete agreed. They slid a hand each under Brian's shoulders and hauled him up the stairs and into Pete's bedroom. There was only a single chair and one of the biggest beds you could imagine in the room, and they laid Brian down on the bed.

"You fancy having some fun tonight Pete," she asked him hopefully.

"Not tonight Mo, I need to sleep and I'm really not in the mood for crumpet tonight."

"Fair enough, we'll just sleep then. Help me get Bri's kit off and we'll all crash in your bed."

The two of them started to undress Brian, he was a dead weight and they had to roll him over to get his trousers off, he made no resistance and there was no signs of him waking up anytime soon. He was lying there in his underpants and Mona said, "I gotta get a look at what Brenda's always bragging about," and she pulled of his boxer shorts.

"Holy shit!" Mona exclaimed, "you know I see a lot of cocks in my line of work Pete, but I've never seen one as healthy as that. It's fucking huge, just look at it."

"Pete gasped, "Oh my! I had no idea he was that well equipped, it's gorgeous."

"I can't leave it like that," Mona said and looked around the room. On the single chair was a box of chocolates with a red ribbon on the lid. She took off the ribbon and walked back to the bed where she proceeded to tie it around Brian's penis and testicles, finishing off with a beautiful bow.

"There, that's what a dick like that deserves," and she pushed him under the covers.

Pete and Mona took off their clothes and climbed into the bed as well, this was not the first time they had shared the bed together and not even the first time they had shared it with another person, but tonight she pecked his cheek, said "Goodnight hun," and they both fell sound asleep.

The next morning, Chud's got a panicky phone call from the under-manager of the Bingo Hall. Brian had been supposed to be there to let the cleaning crew in because his deputy was away visiting family. Promising to deal with it Chuds called Brian's house and Brenda said he hadn't come home. She did not sound pleased either, Chuds assured her not to worry and said he'd probably just had too much to drink at the pub, he promised to go there and check.

He drove over to the pub and banged on the public bar door until a cleaner answered. He asked if anyone was sleeping upstairs, the cleaner shrugged her shoulders and went back to mopping the sticky bar floor.

Making his way up the winding stairs he was hoping that Brian was okay. In the public entertainment business it was always possible to make enemies and Chud's mind was racing with possibilities, but he was not prepared for what he saw when he walked into the bedroom. Brian, Mona and Pete were all asleep, all appeared to be naked and all were in the bed together.

Chuds walked over and shook Brian's shoulder violently, it took a while, but his friend's eyes gradually began to open. Consciousness slowly returned and Brian muttered through a dry mouth, "Chuds. What's going on?"

He looked to his right and saw the huge naked body of Fat Mona, and lying next to her was and equally naked Poncy Pete.

"What the fuck?" and he jumped out of the bed, standing there naked.

"Chuds, what happened, I remember us all drinking then this?"

His voice made Mona and Pete wake up, and Pete kissed her cheek then looked at Brian and said "Morning lover, how are you today?"

Brian's jaw dropped, he shook his head slowly until his hangover made that too painful.

"Chuds, I gotta get out of here," he looked for his clothes, then looked down at his penis and saw the red ribbon tied in a bow around his genitals.

Chuds looked over at the bed and saw Pete and Mona sitting up now. Mona's huge breasts were hanging over the duvet cover and she was smiling at Brian. Chuds nodded towards them and asked his hungover friend, "Did you?"

"I don't know what I did or didn't do Chuds, but it looks like my todjer won first prize."

He grabbed his clothes and went to the bathroom, Mona looked at Chuds and patted the bed beside her.

"Wanna ride Chuds?"

"Not today Mona, I got work to do."

"Okay big boy, but if you change your mind let me know. Free to you, of course."

"I appreciate that Mona, but we gotta get going."

"Before you go Chuds," she paused, "pass those choccies on the chair over here."

Chapter 11

"I don't think it was that Chuds. In fact I still got that piece of ribbon, quite proud of it.. I was in the Army for a while, you know, while you was gone."

Ronnie gulped hard and some of his beer went back into the glass.

"Brian, you was in the territorial Army. The closest you got to any action was visiting a whore house in Southampton while on a training weekend."

"Still could have been it Ronnie. You don't know. You wasn't there."

"The only Trauma you experienced there was spending five hundred quid on prossies."

Chuds thought about the conversation. About the inanity of it all. What had happened to his friends while he was gone? Obviously his first priority was to sort himself out, but he then had to find a way to reverse this malaise that seemed to be slowly creeping over his old crew. Ronnie seemed okay, pretty much the same as when he'd left the country, but Brian was close to a basket case. Looking at his old friend he asked him how Brenda was doing.

"She left me Chuds. I'm not easy to live with, this Past Dramatic is terrible for a relationship."

"Look Brian, I just got back and I need to sort myself out first, but let's see if we can get you back in form after that shall we?"

"Not sure I'm savable Chuds, but I'd appreciate anything you can do to help me out."

"Ronnie, I have work tomorrow thanks to you, any chance you can run me back to my daughter's place."

"Sure thing Chuds, let's finish our bevvies and we'll head right out."

Chapter 12

After spending a quiet evening at his daughter's house and some great bonding time playing with the grand kids, Chuds slept well. The stress of not having a job was lifted and he could already see a way forward. The meeting with Brian had upset him, but he felt confident that with some purpose in his life his old friend could pull himself up again.

He had been a great team member in the past. When Chuds had bought the old Bingo hall from the chain that wanted to release it, he had kept Brian on as manager. The facility was popular but wasn't making enough money for the big guys to keep it running. Chuds and Brian had worked out a way to increase the prize money and draw in more customers, then they started to use some of the rooms out the back to run a few sideline operations.

Chuds' Uncle Jeff was a docker and had quite a history of 'sampling' some of the containers.

A year previously Chuds had gone to his Uncle's semi-detached house and while talking had mentioned that he needed to buy a new kettle.

"No need to buy one young'un, come round to the garage."

As they walked around, Uncle Jeff rolled up the shutter on the garage door. There was no room for a car in there, it was packed to the ceiling with appliances, non-perishable foodstuffs and even a pallet of brief cases.

"What the hell Uncle Jeff. You storing stuff for Argos on the side?"

"Just a few bits that fell out the back of a container or two at the docks Chuds."

"A few bits! Come on Uncle, you've got enough to open a super market here."

"That's the trouble Chuds. I know how to get it home, don't know what to do with it after that though."

"I might be able to help you there Unc. Now, you got a kettle in there?"

Brian and Chuds had gotten Ronnie to bring his van round and they had loaded it up with a healthy sampling of the contraband, and moved it to the Bingo Hall.

Brian had started running raffles, then super-raffles and over the course of a few weeks they had doubled the take, Uncle Jeff was seeing a return on his efforts and soon the raffles were paying the mortgage. Brian's salary went up and that was just one of the ways he had proved himself as a team player and valuable crew member.

Chuds wanted **that** Brian back, the thinker, the doer, not the whining defeated man he had met yesterday.

There was time though, first things first, he had get back on his own two feet so, after playing with the kids a little more and having had a nice lunch, he took the bus into the town centre and arrived at Giovanni's around 3:30.

The restaurant was closed but inside he could see a lady vacuuming the floor and a couple of people setting out tables. Tapping on the glass door he attracted their attention and soon one opened the door. He explained that he was starting there as a dishwasher and was reporting for work, the lady just ushered him in, sat him at a table and told him to wait for Mr. Steve.

He waited patiently, one of his many skills. He didn't need to stare at a phone screen to pass the time, he simply sat, watched the cleaners without being intimidating, and also kept an eye on the members of the public that walked by the large windows of the restaurant.

"Better than TV," he muttered quietly.

Right around 4:00 Steve turned up and shook Chuds' hand firmly.

"Welcome to the crazy world of Giovanni's Chuds, good to have you on board."

"Pleasure to be here Steve, and thanks again for the job."

"Come out to the kitchen, you know how to work an espresso machine?"

"Funnily enough I do Steve."

"Make a couple of doubles and I'll give you the grand tour."
Chuds walked over to the machine and pulled some ground coffee into the puck. Tamping it down he placed two small white cups under the spouts and hit the brew button. The coffee started to trickle out and while Chuds kept an eye on the temperature and the pressure he took in a deep breath through his nose, savouring the smell of freshly brewed espresso.

Once the cycle was finished he took off the puck and banged out the grounds into a small bin. Putting the cups onto two white saucers he carried them over to Steve and they both drank their espresso standing outside of the kitchen area,

"Nice job Chuds. If we need a barista anytime I know who to call."

"Anything you need Steve, I am truly grateful for the job and I'll help any way that I can."

"Come on, I'll show you the whole place."

They walked through the kitchen area, Steve identifying the stations and pointing out the compost bins, the trash bins and the recycling bins, and the huge sinks for dishwashing.

"This will be your new kingdom Chuds, you sure that you're okay doing this job?"

"Ask me again in a few weeks Steve, but yeah, I'm happy to do anything."

"Here, I'll show you upstairs, there's a little staff break room and an area that you might be interested in."

They walked up the wooden stairs to the first floor and Steve pointed out the break room, the staff toilets and then showed him a small room with a single cot bed inside and a small wardrobe.

"Ronnie vouched for you Chuds, so if you're interested you can use this room until you can get your own place, and there's no rush on that either. It'll be good to have someone sleeping on the premises, kind of added security. You can use the back entrance to the restaurant and come and go as you please."

"Steve, if you're sure, I'd love it."

"Very sure Chuds, let's go back down, the staff will be arriving soon and we'll prep for this evening."

As Chuds started to wipe down the sinks and draining areas and placing bags into the bins the kitchen and waiting staff started to arrive. Steve dutifully introduced them all and finally the head cook arrived.

"Chuds, this is our head cook, sometimes he even calls himself a chef, he likes to be called Antonio."

"Pleasure to meet you Antonio," and Chuds put out a hand. The chef shook his hand and said in return, "Gooda evening, itsa pleasure to meet you," in some weird Italian accent. Not being well versed enough to identify the region Chuds simply smiled and went back to tidying his work area.

Steve came back over and explained that they did open for lunch but foot traffic was light. They only opened half of the floor space and it was about 50/50 with dine in and take out orders. The lunchtime crew did their own cleaning and 2 ladies came in after lunch to get the restaurant ship shape for the evening, which was when the real business happened.

Once everything was ready and the wait staff had the tables made up everyone took a short break and waited for the customers to roll in.

It seemed there was two distinct groups of customers that came to the restaurant in the evening. The early shift which was mainly families with kids, then a change as the night crowd came in. These people were either on the way somewhere, had just left somewhere or Giovanni's WAS the where.

Various shades of "tom-drunkery" as Steve called it, with of course the late night crowd being potentially the most dangerous.

"We put reserved notices on every table after 11:00 pm Chuds. Then if people come to the door and look too far gone and present too much potential for tom-drunkery, we just don't let them in."

"Sounds sensible to me," Chuds replied.

"Okay, it's 6:00 pm, the girls will flip the door sign, let's see what tonight brings."

It turned out that the night brought a steady stream of customers. As Steve had predicted the early crowd were families, lots of pasta dishes and family sized pizzas, which came out of the huge pizza oven smelling so good. The kids filled themselves on soda drinks the parents on beer or soft cordials and the whole atmosphere was pleasant.

As the dishes came back from the wait staff Chuds used the flat of his hand and slid it across the plates to put the food waste into the compost ready bins, the knives and forks went into a large sink to soak and the plates were stacked in the next sink. As soon as one table was cleared he washed the plates thoroughly, front and back, rinsed them and placed them in the drainer. Then got to the cutlery which he washed in boiling hot water, "thank goodness for the Marigolds" he muttered on more than one occasion as the thick rubber gloves protected his hands from the water's heat. They too drained and he wiped down the area after every table load.

Steve had been keeping an eye on his work and was suitably impressed. He recognized the attitude of a man that did everything with 100% attention to detail, and silently hoped that Chuds didn't tire of the job too quickly.

The late evening crowd was more boisterous, wine was poured, shots were delivered and copious amounts of food were ordered. The dishes arrived quickly and Chuds maintained his rhythm, there was seldom a backlog of dirty plates and his area stayed clean all night.

The kitchen staff worked well together, only the man who liked to be called Antonio made much noise, as he yelled out orders and directed the plating. His accent was bizarre, but Chuds didn't want to ask anyone about it yet. The staff complied though, but nobody ever replied "Yes Chef", they just carried on with their work. It was truly impressive the speed at which orders were completed, and the wait staff came and whisked plates away only to bring them back half empty an hour or so later.

As the evening wound down, Steve came over to Chuds and complimented him on his dish washing prowess.

"You had that station running like clockwork Chuds."
"Clockwork Orange more like," Chuds retorted with a smile.

"This a typical mid week evening Steve?"

"Yeah, it gets a lot busier at the weekend when we have some live music though," Steve replied.

"I'll definitely take you up on that room then, I'll bring some clothes in tomorrow."

"Fair enough, and thanks for a great evening's work. You need any cash as an advance Chuds?"

"No, I'm good, thanks Steve. Ronnie said he'd take me to my kid's place tonight and then from tomorrow I'll kip here."

"Good deal, the last people are about to leave and we'll close up. At the weekends we sometimes stay on a bit and party for a while, you will of course be welcome to join in."

"I look forward to that, Thanks again Steve."

Chapter 13

Chuds got a really good sleep that night. Although the previous evening's work hadn't been too physical, it had tired him enough to provide a solid eight hours of rest and he woke feeling really refreshed. Over breakfast with the family he explained the spare restaurant room deal and packed a small bag with clothes, toiletries and a couple of books. His daughter offered to drive him into town but Chuds decided to walk until a bus came along.

The day was cold but bright, his daughter's place was what his father would have called "out in the country" and the air smelled clean and felt fresh on his face. Throwing the bag over his shoulder he set out to walk the nine miles, or catch a bus if one came. However, about three miles into his hike a car pulled up beside him, and the passenger side window rolled down.

Looking carefully inside the vehicle, Chuds saw a man in his early thirties, black hair oiled back with mid length sideburns. He had "designer stubble" which Chuds personally hated and he was smoking a cigarette which had filled the car interior with smoke.

"Mr. Douglas," his accent was Eastern European but his English very good, "Can I give you a ride?"

"Do I know you?" Chuds asked. However he already knew that the answer was no, he had never seen this man in his life, so how did he know his name?

"No, I am a friend of Steve's at the restaurant, I thought maybe you would appreciate a ride instead of walking."

Chuds quickly assessed the situation. The man had used his real name instead of the name that everyone knew him by, and he had obviously been waiting around his daughter's place to see when Chuds would leave for work. This did not seem kosher at all.

"It's okay, I really want some fresh air, the walk will be good for me, besides with no judgement, you car is a little smokey for me," and Chuds started to continue his walk.

The car edged along beside him and the man called through the open window.

"Mr. Douglas, I really would like to talk to you. I have a message from my father and he will not like it if I don't deliver it to you."

"Do I know your father then?" Chuds asked.

"I don't think so, but he knows of you Mr. Douglas. Please get in the car."

"There are two chances of that happening, none and fuck all," Chuds continued his walk and the car continued to shadow him along the small country road.

Finally it pulled ahead of him and then parked about 50 feet in front. The driver got out of the vehicle and Chuds braced as the man walked towards him.

"Why are you making this unpleasant Mr. Douglas?"

"I thought I had been the personification of good manners," Chuds paused, "So far."

The man put a hand into his jacket pocket, Chuds took note to see if he could tell what the man was reaching for. Best case scenario a phone, worst case a gun, more likely, if the man was from Eastern Europe, a knife.

He kept walking towards Chuds who stayed still.

"Mr. Douglas. My father wants to know why you are back in town. He does his research and he knows that many years ago, you were like the King of...."

"I was never a king of anything," Chuds interrupted, "Just a business man with interests in a lot of things."

The man kept walking and his hand was still in his pocket, when he was about 3 feet away from Chuds he stepped forward quickly, put his left leg in front of the walking man and put his right hand on the back of his head and turned left quickly, pushing him face first into the road. He followed through and pushed his knee dead centre of the man's back, pinning him in place. Grabbing the man's right arm he yanked it from the jacket pocket and a medium sized knife, still closed, clattered to the ground. Chuds pushed it away and placed his head close to the man's ear.

"As I said," Chuds' voice was calm, controlled, firm, "I've been the personification of good manners, up until now. Tell your dad I'm just trying to get my life back in order, I am not interested in anything he's up to and if he wants to talk to me, don't send the idiot son."

The man writhed under Chuds' knee but the body weight plus the pressure on his head kept him in place.

Chuds continued, "I just want to be left alone, catch up with some old friends and decide what to do next with my life. Just leave me alone, understand?"

The pinned man grunted and dirt from the road entered his mouth, making him cough.

"That was what we call a rhetorical question, I'm sure that you understand, I'm sure that your dad will be upset and I really don't fucking care. Now get in your car and drive home like a good son."

He brought his knee up and stood up quickly staying on alert. The grounded man stood up, glaring at Chuds, but not keen to continue the conversation. He backed towards his car, and Chuds called out, "Hey, no littering," and pointed at the knife. As the man carefully stepped forward to pick it up he never took his eyes from his opponents face, then he backed to the car, got into the driver's seat and pulled away quickly.

"Some mother's kids," Chuds muttered. He picked his bag up and carried on walking. Hopefully that will be the end of any problems, but he had no reference for the level of their stake in the town's soft white underbelly or what they would do to protect it.

He hadn't lied, he really had no interest in getting back into his old ways, he just wanted to wait and see what opportunities would come along.

Eventually the country back road merged with the main road that led to the town centre. Traffic became busier, the fresh county air changed to the smell of carbon monoxide but still it was a nice walk, and maintained a steady pace.

Another car pulled up beside him and the window rolled down, just like before.

"Not again," Chuds sighed but looked into the car's interior anyway. He saw a woman, mid 40's, long brown hair, smartly dressed with fashionable glasses. This was a definite upgrade on his last encounter.

The woman looked at him and said, "Chuds? Is that you?"

"Depends, do I owe you money?" Chuds grinned.

"I don't think so. Maybe an apology or two but I don't think you owe me any money. Need a ride?"

"I don't really need one, but I'll take one," he paused and looked carefully at the driver, "You look familiar but I'm really sorry, I've been away a for quite a while and I just don't recognize you."

"Climb in, we'll catch up," and she unlocked the door with a button on the dashboard.

He got into the passenger seat, put the seat belt on and the car pulled away, heading towards the town centre.

"So, Chuds. Still no idea who I am?"

Turning his head to the woman he looked carefully at her, "Sorry, but no. As I said you look so familiar but I'm drawing a blank."

"Oh Chuds," her voice was low but soft and her accent was definitely local. "Remember being in a band with Andy, back in the day and playing a gig at that pub hall in Chatham? Really big for you boys at the time, must have been a couple of hundred people there."

"I sure do, were you there that night too?"

"Kind of... My name's Martina, or Marti... think carefully Chuds."

Chapter 14

20th February 1981 – The Big Gig

The hall that was annexed onto the White Horse pub in Chatham had over 200 people in it, all milling around, sipping their beers or mixed drinks, the conversations were overlapping, and everyone had paid a small cover charge to hear the band.

Meanwhile, backstage in the green room, which had previously been a large cleaning closet, the five members of Suspicious Biscuit were tuning their guitars and running through the set list. This was one of Andy's bands and Chuds Douglas was subbing on bass once again, "just until a real one comes along," as Andy would say.

This was probably the largest crowd they had ever played to, usually they were crammed into the corner in some bar lounge, but tonight they had a stage, with actual curtains and had even invested in a smoke machine and a couple of strobe lights to beef up the performance. The band were all dressed in regular street clothes except for the singer, Martin, who was channelling his best Freddie Mercury. He was wearing a white vest and blue Levi jeans, his face had carefully trimmed beard stubble and his hair was smoothed down with what seemed to be a whole jar of Brylcreem.

"You're looking, err, I don't know what to say, different?" Andy said, but it was time to go on, so they all walked onto the stage.

The front of house lights dimmed and the crowd started to cheer. Andy looked over at Ronnie in the wings, nodded, and he flicked the switch on the dry ice machine, two extraction hoses from washing machines pushed the smoke over to each side of the stage and started to fill the whole stage floor. Low red lighting flooded the performance area and Andy, Chuds and Martin stepped up to their mics.

Andy quietly counted in.. "Two..Three" and the three men started singing the harmonies from the opening of "Since you've been gone" by Rainbow.

The arrangement was different from the original, and started with the opening lines sung acapella in three part harmony, Ronnie was to open the curtain on the sixth line just as they all sang the "Oh oh oh oh, Oh oh oh oh..." part and the smoke would hopefully stream out over the stage as Martin walked to the front, they would all finished the chorus with "Ever since you've been gone," to be followed by a gutteral, sexually charged "UH!" from Martin. Then the instrumental would come in loud and they would steam into the first verse.

That was the plan.

What happened went exactly as planned, right up until the "Uh."

Martin had been told to really sell the "Uh" sound. Andy had tried so hard to get him to understand the concept, "It should be like you're giving it to a girl, right at the end let it all out with a loud and deep and sexy "UH", bring it right up from the diaphragm."

Martin nodded his understanding, told Andy not to worry, told him that he'd got it but kept fixing his hair in the backstage mirror.

So the harmonies started, Ronnie set the smoke running, dimmed the lights to Valentine Red and on line 6 opened up the curtains. The smoke rolled over the front of the stage and the three singers hit perfect pitch as the song started up. Martin picked up the mic stand and strode purposefully to the front of the stage.

As the three men finished the line "Ever since you've been gone," he paused, looked at the front row of cheering punters and let out an "oo" noise that sounded like Frankie Howard on a good day. A soft, effeminate "oo" that was waiting for the rest of the "oo missus, titter ye not" to follow.

Tom the drummer stopped immediately and yelled "OO?" What the fuck's "OO?" and collapsed over his kit laughing. Andy and Chuds joined in the laughter until they realized that the biggest crowd of their short career was waiting expectantly for the song to continue.

Tom hit his sticks together three times and the song amazingly started up again, and finished to a rousing cheer. The rest of the set went as planned, some covers, a few originals and an obligatory drum solo. After the encore they all went back to the green room/cleaning closet. Martin was visibly upset and Andy looked at him and said, "Martin, this isn't going to work out. We'll get a new singer."

Choking back tears Martin said, "Are you firing me because I'm gay?"

"Nope! Didn't know you're gay, I'm firing you because you sing like you're gay."

He stormed out with his duffel bag of street clothes, and the band never saw him again.

Chapter 15

"That was me Chuds. I was Martin back in those days, I'm TS and live as a woman now."

"Fucking hell Marti, that's a turn up. A very good looking woman if I can say that."

"You can Chuds, you can."

There was a long silence in the car as Marti drove them to the top of the High Street.

"I'd love to really catch up Marti, have you tell me all about things that I really don't understand, if that's okay with you."

"Sure Chuds, I'd love that," and she handed him a business card that promoted her as Marti, Jazz, Swing and Pop Singer for your important event, "Do you still play bass guitar?"

"I wouldn't know which way round to hold it after all this time Marti."

He stepped out of the car and looking back in he said, "I'll call you Marti, thanks for the ride," and he walked down the sloping street towards the restaurant.

The afternoon cleaning crew let him in once again and he went upstairs to set up the small room, and when Steve arrived he gave him a key for the back door to the restaurant. He told Steve about the run in with the guy in the car, and it didn't seem to concern him too much.

"Chuds, if even I knew who you are, they are bound to know. Probably just sabre rattling, if you know what I mean."

"Yeah, I just hope it doesn't come here. He first presented himself as a friend of yours so they must know I'm working for you. If it creates any problems I'll just walk away, but I must admit, I do enjoy this job. Very meditative."

"Don't let it worry you too much, the old man himself comes in here sometimes, I'll reach out and ask them to back off."

"I'd appreciate that Steve, shall we get the place ready for the evening crowd?"

With that the two men went down to the kitchen and Chuds started to get his work area ready as well as cleaning a lot of the preparation surfaces. Despite Steve telling him that it was not necessary he carried on anyway, until the kitchen and wait crew arrived.

The next few days flew by for Chuds. He worked the dishwashing section of the restaurant, had lunch there as well and took a few walks around the town. He was amazed at how much had changed and yet loved how so much of the historical buildings had been preserved. At one time the town had boasted of more pubs per head of population than any other town in the country, but many of them were now shops, restaurants or homes.

The menswear shop where he had bought his first ever suit was now a Costa Coffee Shop and one of the largest and oldest pubs in the town centre was now a McDonalds fast food joint. He also went into the small coffee shop a few times where he had first met the girl with the big ear piercings and the bad attitude, she gave no indication of remembering him and certainly hadn't improved her people skills. It was, however, a nice place to sit and watch the world go by and she did make a nice cup of coffee.

The weekend rolled around and as Chuds was preparing for the evening's work a man was setting up a small amp and mic near the coffee bar area, obviously the live entertainment for the night. Chuds went over introduce himself and the two men struck up a conversation for a while. The singer's stage name was Jonny Mowton and he worked every weekend at Giovanni's "trying to be heard above the noise" and playing pop classics and ballads.

At 6:00 they opened the doors and the families slowly rolled in, the work was very much like the weekdays and there was no problem keeping up with the flow of dishes, but at 8:00 as the music started the crowd changed. It was date night for sure, and drinking night definitely. The restaurant filled and as soon as a table was cleaned another group sat down.

The kitchen was hot and Chuds was amazed at how the staff kept the food flowing out to the restaurant with very little delay. The man who likes to be called Antonio barked out instructions and while still nobody replied "Yes Chef" they followed the instructions and the plates kept leaving the kitchen, only to return about an hour later for cleaning.

They could hear the music filtering through to the kitchen and Mr. Mowton seemed to have a good repertoire and great lines of patter. Laughter punctuated the songs and Chuds just knew that was making the bar receipts go up. There was definitely a great atmosphere in the restaurant, and at 9:30 the singer took a break and came back to the kitchen for some food. He and Chuds chatted for a while as the plates came through. Jonny told him that the drinkers would start arriving soon, but generally everything was okay, sometimes loud and often boisterous but seldom "fighty."

"Fighty, I like that word," Chuds replied.

Sure enough the noise from the restaurant got louder, the music's volume increased to match and gradually there was a lot of singing from the crowd. The slight lull in food orders finished and the kitchen was cranked up to full capacity. It was hard work but Chuds kept the dishes and glasses clean and even managed to keep his work services clean. By the end of the evening there was only the utensils and pots and pans and finally it was finished.

Steve walked into the kitchen, congratulated everyone and yelled, "Lock In! First round is on me."

The kitchen crew and the wait staff cheered and everyone went through to the restaurant for some drinks. People who had only known Chuds as "the new dishwasher" came and chatted and everybody wound down. Steve was busy counting the receipts and putting the money in the safe, although most people paid by card nowadays apparently, and the atmosphere was relaxed and fun.

Jonny Mowton sang a couple of songs as did some of the staff, and it was soon approaching 2:00 am when a loud knocking started at the front door. The chatter died down a little and Steve went to investigate, he pulled the blind to one side and saw a very angry woman, who was yelling, "Is he here? Is he?"

Steve yelled back, "We're closed" but she kept banging at the door until Steve opened it a crack. That was his first mistake and she pushed by him, looking around the staff as if hunting prey.

"Where is he, I know he's here. Come out you bastard."

Finally, the man who likes to be called Antonio emerged form the kitchen, he already looked defeated and the woman rounded on him.

"You said no more of this. You've got kids at home that call you Uncle Daddy, you promised no more late, late nights, now get your coat you bastard you're coming home right now."

"Whya you talka to me thata way, Ima the chef here,"

"Shut the fuck up and stop using that accent. You're not Italian, that accent's not even Italian, you just work in an Italian Restaurant and your names Alfred. Now get your fucking coat and come home with me NOW!"

The man who liked to be called Antonio hung his head and walked back to the kitchen area to get his coat. As he came back and followed his wife to the restaurant door, he looked back at his co-workers.

"I'lla see you alla tomorrow."

"Good Night Alfred!!!" the crew yelled in unison and Steve locked the door behind them.

"One more round, on me, then you can all fuck off home," Steve called out and the crew cheered again.

Chapter 16

Friday and Saturday were definitely the busiest nights at Giovanni's, Sunday a little less so and at the end of the week Steve gave Chuds his first pay packet. Without opening the envelope he put it straight into his pocket and shook the man's hand.

"Not gonna count it Chuds?"

"I don't think I need to Steve," and he grinned.

"Tuesday is our quietest day, why don't you take it off Chuds? You must be tired."

"Sounds great, I'd like to catch up with a few people."

The next day he called Ronnie and asked him to get any of the old crew that still wanted to talk to him together for lunch.

"Does Poncy Pete still run a boozer?"

"He does Chuds, still down by the River, but it's full of poofters these days. Full on gay bar nowadays Chuds."

"His pub was always a gay bar Ronnie."

"It was? Fuckin' hell how did I miss that?"

"Let's all have lunch there, noon on Tuesday, I miss that old fairy."

Charles Douglas Senior, also known as Chuds' dad, had only ever imparted three pearls of wisdom to his son. These were:

1. Never let a woman see you in just your socks and pants (and NEVER just your socks)
2. Never pick a fight that you have no hope of winning
3. On time is late, 5 minutes early is on time

He had never broken any of these rules, although he had bent number 2 a couple of times, but he was a stickler for punctuality. At 11:55 he walked through the doors of "The Russian's Arms" and stepped straight up to the bar.

As he had entered his eyes scanned the room, but he didn't recognize any of the old faces and none of the new ones looked suspicious. The barmaid was big, very big, she had her back to the bar while she was polishing the counter below the optics, but she caught Chuds' reflection in the mirror and spun around to greet him.

"As I live and breathe, Chuds Douglas!"

Fat Mona had aged well. Her face looked pretty much the same as when Chuds had last seen her almost 20 years ago. Maybe she had gained a few pounds, it was hard to tell really, but her smile was exactly the same and her eyes shone as she eyed Chuds up and down.

"Chuds, you're a sight for sore eyes and sight for open thighs. If I was 20 years younger and half a stone lighter I'd jump the bar and jump your bones."

"It's good to see you Mona, a few of the old crew may be coming in for lunch, you still do pub grub?"

"I can get Pete to do some sarnies, if that's okay?"

"Perfect Mona, and I'll have a pint of Guinness while we're waiting."

Mona walked to the end of the bar, looked up a flight of stairs and yelled, "Pete! You old ponce, an old friend of yours is in the bar, but don't you dare come down without a tray of assorted sarnies."

A high pitched and very affected voice yelled back down, "Who is it Mona? What kind of Sarnies?"

She looked at Chuds and mouthed, "Cheese and Pickled Onion?" Chuds nodded and she shouted the order up the stairs.

"Cheese and Pickled Onion? Is that Chuds Fucking Douglas in the bar?"

The footsteps pounded on the stairs and what was perhaps the skinniest man in the world swung around the doorway, put his hands to his throat and screamed, "Clutch the pearls! Chuds where have you been?"

"Had a bit of trouble in the States Poncy, they threw me out, just getting back on my feet in the old home town."

Poncy Pete had genuine tears in his eyes and he blew Chuds a kiss, "Mona will take care of you I'll make the sandwiches."

"Oh I'll take care of him alright," and Mona winked at Chuds.

"Behave yourself you fat slag, I don't pay you to flirt with the punters."

"Oh, I'd do this one for free Pete, now fuck off and let me enjoy myself."

Mona poured the Guinness and started to make small talk. The pub only had a few people in, most sitting at tables and a couple on stools at the bar.

"Everything okay in here Mo? Anyone I need to be nervous of?"

"Chuds, I don't think anyone here knows who you are or who you were. Most of these are regulars, couple of new faces up by the dartboard, you're all okay."

"Somebody knows who I am, some Eastern European type fronted me the other day. It had the potential to get nasty but it all seems to have blown over."

"Relax lover, I'll keep an eye on things. Anyone steps out of line I'll fucking sit on them."

"Do they have to pay extra for that?" Chuds winked at her.

"I still turn a few tricks now and then Chuds. There's still enough chubby chasers and at my age I can't outrun the bastards any more. Not that I ever tried too much. My daughter does most of the legwork now. She says business is so good if she had another pair of legs, she'd open them in Dartford as well."

"A daughter Mona? Wow we have some catching up to do as well."
"She's a good girl Chuds, works in a coffee shop that Pete and I own up the High Street."

"Really? Big holes in the ear lobes?"

"That's her, you met? She's a good girl, sort of."

"Bit surly? Yeah I met her Mona, I wouldn't say we hit it off right away but I've been in there a few times and she hasn't attacked me yet."

"She must really like you then, and who can blame her?"

While they had been chatting, Wrong Way Ronnie and a few friends entered the bar. Chuds watched them in the reflection of the mirror behind the bar but didn't turn around until Ronnie tapped him on the shoulder.

"Afternoon chaps, thanks for coming, I can't wait to catch up with you all. First rounds on me, but as I've only had one pay packet since I got back, it's every man for himself after that."

As Mona poured the beers, Ronnie carried them to the table. Brian was looking about as depressed as he had been the last time Chuds saw him and he was sitting with TGT, Big Steve and Nobby. Once everyone had a beer in their hands Chuds raised his glass and said, "Cheers!"

The gesture was returned by everyone and Chuds walked to the table and sat down. The small talk started. Everyone wanted to know about the deportation and what Chuds had been doing in the States. Poncy Pete brought the sandwiches to the table, squeezed Chuds' shoulder and minced away, much to Ronnie's disgust.

"Poofter," Ronnie muttered.

Chuds shot him a "Not now," look and Ronnie lowered his head.

As the men tucked in to the sandwiches and the conversation flowed Chuds noticed his old colleague Nobby constantly looking at a weird watch on his wrist. This made him a little nervous and he wondered if Nobby was expecting someone. Nobby had worked for him, but they weren't exactly close and it would not have surprised him if he had tipped someone off that Chuds was going to be in the pub at a certain time. He was probably being paranoid but after the incident on the road the other day, he didn't want to take too many chances.

"What's with the watch checking Nobby? Expecting someone?"

"Oh no Chuds, s'not a watch, it's one of them fitness trackers. Keeps a total of how many steps you do every day and tracks your heartbeat and everything."
"Nobby, you're sitting at a table in a pub, your steps aren't going to increase, maybe Fat Mona's making your heart rate go up?"

"Leave it out Chuds. It's just a force of habit that I keep checking it. It's a really good device. Here, not a lot of people know this, but if you're 'aving it off every stroke counts as a step. I gave the missus a real good seein' to last night, I mean a real headboard rattler and I don't want to brag but I checked this afterwards and I had a whole 4 extra steps!"

"She's a lucky woman Nobby, a lucky woman indeed."

Chuds took a long sip from the Guinness and let out a long sigh. A couple of the guys asked if he had any plans to get back into the old businesses, which although he didn't rule anything out he emphasised to all of them that he had no plans laid out at all.

"Guys, I'm taking it one day at a time, I have no plans, in fact I'm still just trying to find my feet again, it's hard being picked up and dropped off into a place you haven't seen for almost 2 decades."

The guys mostly nodded, and let Chuds know what they had been up to, Fat Mona kept the beers coming and Poncy Pete fluttered around like an elderly butterfly. It was a harmless lunchtime get together, but Chuds couldn't help but feel uneasy after the run in a few days earlier. He kept an eye on everyone that came in and out of the pub to see if they paid his group too much attention.

TGT, Two Gears Tony told him he had taken a partnership in a small taxi firm. Despite being one of the worst drivers you could ever meet he had always made his living driving, he just hated changing gears.

"How many clutches have you burnt out in the taxi fleet TGT?"

"Oh, you know, a few Chuds."

"Ever thought of switching to an automatic?"

"What's that then Chuds, like a self-driving car?"

"You fucking wish Tony. Seriously though you'd save a fortune if you switched from a manual to an auto."

"Nah, I like 'aving the control Chuds."

"The fuck you do Tony, you only use 2 gears and that's not really control is it?"

"It's enough for me Chuds. Anyway, I didn't ask you for business advice did I?"

"Fair enough Tony, just trying to help."

Looking around the group, it really represented only a handful of the people that had worked with him over the years. He nodded at Big Steve, who was all of 5ft 2 inches tall, and asked what he was up to nowadays. It seemed that Steve had stuck with the girly business. He had taken over the massage parlours and it was all going well for a while. Looking over his shoulder at Fat Mona he nodded towards Steve and raised his eyebrows questioningly. Mona nodded, so it seemed that she had helped him at some time.

Following on from the few parlours that Chuds had owned before he left the country, Steve had opened a couple more and maintained the image that had served them so well. Decent and discrete signage outside and an air of respectability that lasted from the moment you walked in the door to the moment you laid on the table.

Every parlour had nice showers, a well decorated lounge area, a polite and well spoken receptionist and beautifully designed rooms with comfortable massage tables. He also only hired girls who had diplomas in massage therapy so the customers also got a really good massage before the happy ending. When Chuds had run them a few people had tried to compete with them by having cheap everything, but he stuck to his guns and maintained the classy establishments. It worked, the cheap and never-cheerful competitors never lasted long.

The girls also got a percentage of the massage fee and got to keep 90% of the extras, so they made good money, and as word of mouth got around, the parlours stayed pretty busy. There was never a shortage of girls to offer the services and Chuds had always made sure that they were drug and disease free.

"Remember that place we had on the outskirts of Northfleet Chuds?"

Steve sipped his beer.

"Yeah, just off the High Street, right?"

Steve nodded, "A couple of chavs tried opening a place just down the street from us. It was a real shit hole and they kept advertising discounts, but all their advertising was spelled wrong. They kept putting Discunts. Discunts Chuds!"

"What's a Discount massage anyway, like self service? Hand jobs but you have to use your own hand? They lasted a month and the girls there asked for jobs with me, but I sent them packing. Really rough trade."

Apparently over the years while Chuds had been gone, the leaseholds to the spas were gradually taken away. Whenever Steve had tried to renew they were denied and change of use notices issued. One by one the spas disappeared and currently there was only one still operating.

A lot of the property was being bought up by newly arrived European landlords, shops that seemed to sell nothing were at ground level and small apartments and offices were on the upper floors. Several of the old spas were now thinly disguised escort services with a handful of import and export businesses and wholesalers scattered around as well.

It had been a lawful and non-violent eviction, the new tenants had just privately outbid for the leaseholds. Steve looked despondent, he explained that the one spa left was still making money but not nearly enough. What was worse, and this was especially true as far as Chuds was concerned, was that apparently the new escort services were offering "barely legal specials" that were in fact illegal as hell.

"That sounds shocking," Chuds said, "We never once offered anything but good value and girls of a legal age. What's happening to the old town?"

The chats were interspersed with silences as the men sipped their beers, ate their sandwiches and occasionally went outside to smoke. Looking over to Brian, Chuds asked what had happened to the old Bingo Hall. He was dismayed to hear that it was just a totally empty building now.

"When that was a cinema Bri, I saw my first ever movie there. Ben Hur. My old grandad took me and I was 4 or 5 years old. Totally inappropriate film for a kid but I fell in love with the cinema then. I'd love to get that place up and running again Brian. Any chance you can find out who owns the lease now?"

"I can ask around Chuds but does anyone really want to play Bingo now?"

"How about we make it a multi-media venue Brian? Small area for Bingo, a bit for an arcade, a small cinema, couple of hundred seats only. I mean it will be the only one in town, we could make it special. Put a shisha lounge upstairs, come on the possibilities are endless."

"And how would you fund this Chuds? Ain't you washing dishes for a living now?"

"Brian, you gotta make the plan, cost it out then worry about getting the money. Make some calls for me will you?

"S'pose I can Chuds, I'll get on it tomorrow."

As the afternoon grew long, the conversations started to dry up and Chuds began to feel tired.

"Let's call it a day guys, I'm beat. I'll get a phone next week and give Ronnie the number, he can send it out to you all."

He stood and walked over to the bar, "Mona, it's been a treat meeting you again, let's have a sit down soon, maybe in your daughter's cafe? Tell Pete I'll be back soon."

"Chuds, I'm here every weekday from 11:00 am until I get bored or Pete kicks me out. Weekends is for the other business but if YOU ever fancy a bit of the other business, there's a room upstairs we can use," and she winked an exaggerated wink.

"Mo, you're the best. One day I'll take you up on that."

"From your lips to God's ears Chuds Douglas."

He said goodbye again to the guys and walked out of the pub into the late afternoon sunshine. The two men who had been sitting by the dartboard followed him out a minute later and slowly walked after him as he made his way up the High Street towards the restaurant.

Chapter 17

Just because you're paranoid, it doesn't mean they're not out to get you.

Chuds could sense the two guys walking behind him, he had seen them eyeing him a couple of times at the pub. As he got close to Giovanni's he turned down the alley way that led to the back door of the restaurant, but instead of going inside he kept walking and entered the car park at the rear. He bent down in some shadows and pretended to tie his shoelace all the while watching carefully and listening for footsteps.

Finally the two men entered the car park and started to look around, they seemed confused and eventually just gave up and started to walk back down the alley. Chuds stood up and called out, "Hey, guys," and he walked towards them.

"You got a light?" he asked in as friendly a voice as he could muster. He had half hoped that one of the men would be the guy that had tried it on a few days ago, but these two were different. The men looked flustered. It was obvious that their job had been to follow him and just report to someone where he had gone and who he had met with. It did not seem that a confrontation was supposed to be on the agenda.

Chuds did not recognize the accent as the man on the left said, "Sorry, no."

"That's okay, I don't smoke anyway. Guys I'm sure you know where I'm staying for now. I'll go inside and nap for while, you two should probably just jog on."

"Jog on?"

"It means Fuck Off, I was just trying not to be rude."

"You fuck off."

"I intend to do just that fellas, as Number 6 used to say, I'll be seeing you."

The reference to Number 6 sent their confusion levels into overdrive and Chuds went into the restaurant through the back door without ever looking back.

Chuds lay on the bed and drifted into a deep nap. The potential confrontation had defused nicely and the meeting with some of his old friends had been good, there was even some ideas for for the future germinating. After about an hour he woke and decided to wander up to the coffee shop, it was just a few minutes walk from the restaurant and while he had full access to Giovanni's espresso machine he really didn't want to get involved with the restaurant staff on his day off.

Opening the door to the coffee shop, the girl that he now knew to be Fat Mona's daughter briefly looked up from her phone and said, "I'm closing soon."

"Is there time for a quick coffee before you do that?"

"I suppose so," and she stood up to put the kettle on.

"I was just talking to your Mum at the pub."

"Good for you. Milk and sugar? I forget."

"Just black please. I know your Mum from way back, I'm Chuds Douglas, we were business partners of a sort."

"Like I said, good for you."

He took his usual seat by the window and sipped his coffee, watching the people walk by. A few minutes later he saw Ronnie and Mona walking up the High Street, deep in conversation. Tapping on the window he got their attention and called them into the cafe.
"Oy, mind the window you twat."

The girl saw her mother coming in and sighed deeply. "Hello Mum, guess I'm not knocking off after all."

"Nice to see you too Ro," Mona walked to the counter and looking her daughter in the eye said, "He giving you any trouble?" as she nodded towards Chuds.

"None that I can't 'andle"

"I don't doubt that," Mona replied, "You can go home Ro, I've got keys to the place as you know. I'll lock up."

"Fair enough Mum, I'm gonna try my luck at that new hotel down by the river front tonight."

"Good luck Doll, you get any requests for a threesome give your old Mum a call."

"Ew."

Mona's daughter slipped her coat on and left without a goodbye, while Mona herself went behind the counter and made a pot of tea, a second coffee for Chuds and carried everything to the table. Flipping the sign on the door to read "Closed" she joined the two men and poured some tea.

Sipping her tea, she looked over the rim of the cup and said, "Well, isn't this nice?"

The two men nodded and sipped their drinks too. Eventually the conversation started and Chuds asked Mona about her daughter and whether she had married the father.

"Not even sure who the father is Chuds, you know how many men I slept with in my prime?" She laughed heartily, "kind of a math error that one, but she's a good kid despite her hard as nails exterior."

After a few sips of her tea she carried on, "You know, I was the third busiest prossie in the town around the time that you left. Three's a good position to be in Chuds, everyone's gunning to be number 1 while the girl that is number 1 hates the girl that's number 2. I just carried on screwing my chubby chasers and running our small group of girls, I made more money than all of them."

"You still got any of that money Mo?"

"I'm okay Chuds, why? You need a loan?"

"Nah, I'm good Mona but I might be looking for some investors sometime soon."

"Just let me know Chuds, I might be able to help a little. Poncy Pete manages my money but he keeps me up to date on what's what. I think, technically, we're even sitting in my cafe right now."

"Awesome Mona, there's no definite plans just yet but I have a few ideas in my mind."

"Chuds, I'll forever be grateful for the way you helped us out back in the day. You looked after us and if I can help you in return, it would be my pleasure."

They chatted and sipped their drinks until the sun went down. While Chuds had experienced a lot of adventures in his time away, it did feel good to back amongst the people he'd grown up with. Well truthfully, just gotten older, he never did really consider himself to be a grown up.

As Mona locked up the coffee shop and she and Ronnie carried on their walk up the High Street Chuds decided to go back to "The Russian's Arms" and have a final drink with Pete. Nobody followed him this time and he walked into the quiet pub and sat at the bar.

Poncy Pete let out a squeal and minced over to stand opposite Chuds.

"Guinness for you handsome?"

"Sure, thanks Pete."

The 2 old friends sat and chatted for a while, lots of reminiscing, remembering old friends, some of whom had passed on, talking about incidents.

"Chuds, you should come in here on a Saturday night. We have drag acts and singers and the odd comedian. We get a good crowd."

"Busiest night at Giovanni's Pete, those dishes won't wash themselves you know."

"Crying shame you doing a job like that Chuds, with hands like yours you shouldn't be doing dishes."

"Gotta love those Marigolds Pete."

Chapter 18

Wednesday and Thursday were regular working days and Chuds was settling into his daily routine nicely. Friday night rolled around though and the weekend arrived with a bang. Johnny the Musician started setting up and the kitchen staff were all anticipating a busy night, the prep stations were loaded, tables cleaned and set and Steve was floating around checking on everything.

The cleaning stations were ready and Chuds got himself a double espresso to give himself some energy for the evening. On one of his circuits of the restaurant Steve stopped by Chuds' station and told him that the senior man in the local "family business" had a table reserved for the evening.

"I know you've had a couple of run ins with some of the family members Chuds, try not to let anything get out of hand in the restaurant, please."

"Nothing will start from my end Steve, I'll just keep busy washing the dishes."

The family oriented customers started rolling in and the tables started filling up. A large, round table in the corner of the restaurant remained empty with a reserved placard on it, even when people were waiting for a table, until Mr Basha made his appearance. Despite Steve having called him "the Old Man" Basha seemed to be in his late 40's with a handsome face, lined with carefully groomed stubble and dressed in a very nice suit. He took his seat at the table and 2 heavy set men sat either side of him, leaving just one chair next to the patriarch for a guest who presumable would arrive a little later.

Steve himself took the menu over to the table and a waitress brought 3 complimentary glasses of ice water and 1 bottle of cold beer and a glass, which she poured for him, then walked away. The bodyguards looked around but didn't seem totally aware or especially capable to Chuds eyes. The old error of equating size with capability seemed to be in play here.

Eventually he ordered and once the meal arrived he started eating without waiting for whoever was supposed to take the empty seat next to him. Once he had finished his meal Steve took a double espresso over and asked if everything had been okay. Basha nodded his approval and passed over his credit card which Steve brushed away. Telling him that the meal was on the house.

Meanwhile Chuds simply concentrated on keeping up with the dishes which arrived at a fast pace, however he had the station running so smoothly now that there was seldom a backlog. When Basha stood to leave, instead of moving towards the door he walked directly back into the kitchen area and straight over to Chuds.

"Mr. Douglas. My son gave me your message," and he cracked a broad smile.

"I hope I didn't cause you any offence Sir," Chuds replied, "I tried to defuse the situation as easily as I could."

"Mr. Douglas, I didn't send him on any mission, and I believe you were correct in calling him the idiot son. Mr Douglas, or may I call you Chuds?"

Chuds nodded his approval.

"Do I have anything to worry about with your return to this town? We have a nice family business here, and I am hoping that you are not looking to cause me any trouble."

"Mr. Basha, I am sure you have done a little research. I retired from business here many years ago and it is only unfortunate personal circumstances that have made me come back."

"Ah the deportation, yes Mr. Chuds, I heard all about it, and here you are washing dishes. I would say that was unfortunate for you."

Basha spoke well, too well, perfect English with a deliberate attempt to cover any native accent. As he turned to leave he looked back at Chuds and said calmly, "Mr. Douglas. Don't make me worry about you," and he carried on walking out of the kitchen and the restaurant.

"Mr. Douglas? I thought we'd agreed he'd call me Chuds."

Steve came back into the kitchen area to make sure everything was okay, and Chuds assured him that it was.

Outside, in the restaurant, the noise increased, the music got louder and some couples even danced between the tables. The kitchen ran at full steam, with food leaving for the tables constantly and the dishes returning for cleaning. As the last group left, Steve came into the kitchen and thanked everybody for their efforts. He offered a free staff drink after work, but no party tonight. There were a few disappointed grunts but Chuds was looking forward to getting some sleep.

The whole weekend was busy and the time passed very quickly. Chuds received his pay and on Tuesday took another day off.

He had arranged to see the agency that was managing the old Bingo Hall property, and he took Brian with him, thinking that it may fire him up a little and draw him out of his funk. The two men took the train to Waterloo East and walked over to the agency's main office. After a brief wait they were shown into a room and were very quickly joined by one of the agency managers.

Chuds pulled out his new moleskin notebook and explained that his now defunct company had once leased the building and was interested in taking it on again. Explaining how he had tentative plans to convert the building into a multi-media entertainment complex, including a small cinema, e-Bingo, a Shisha lounge and a gaming arcade, he showed the agent some drawings in his notebook.

"We have done some research," and he nodded towards Brian to include him in the conversation, "and while none of those channels of entertainment would support the building by itself, we think that a mix of all of them, and possibly even a couple more outlets would bring value to the town and help to restore the building's previous impressive countenance."

The agent seemed impressed. He informed them that the historical importance of the building was now recognized by none other than British Heritage and that any plans would need to be approved by that organization. The upside of this was that as long as assurances were given to keep the building's previous ambience, the rent would be minimal, subject to approval and a cash guarantee.

"I assure you," Chuds maintained full eye contact and gave the agent his most enigmatic smile, "that building means a lot to me, not because of any past business interests we may have had but because of its importance in my youth. Truthfully, it almost broke my heart when it became a Bingo hall but I think we can bring it up to date while keeping the original facade intact and making any alterations inside of a temporary nature, so as to have no negative impact on the structure."

Once again the agent nodded his approval and told Chuds and Brian that the guarantee would need to be £100,000 but that the rent would be what was known as a peppercorn rent of £1 a year subject to a minimum 10 year contract and the approval of British Heritage.

Chuds signalled his agreement and looked at Brian who had a bemused look on his face. His former best friend was talking about lodging a huge sum of money against a building and committing to a 10 year contract while his only source of income was being made washing dishes at an Italian restaurant. He decided just to nod back and try to look like none of what had just been discussed was impossible.

On the train ride back to Gravesend Chuds asked Brian to get him a cheap smart phone.

"Not too fucking smart Brian, I don't want a device that's smarter than me."

Leafing through his notebook he found some old contacts and checked with Brian whether they were still in the town and available. There were some contractors and one solicitor, an Indian named Anil Singh who had done a lot of legal work for Chuds previously.

"Yeah, old Anil is still around, I think he has a pretty big law firm now Chuds, by Gravesend standards anyway."

That information brought a smile to Chuds' face and he made a large tick by an entry in his notebook.

"Brian, once we decide for sure what we're going to put in there we'll subcontract each area to someone we trust and get rents from them on their individual operations. I think Fat Mona might run the shisha lounge with a coffee shop and a VIP room, and pay us rent on her area. We can limit our financial exposure while collecting rents from the operators."

"Sounds lovely Chuds, where you gonna get 100K though?"

"Leave that to me Bri," and he tapped the side of his nose.

Chapter 19

The next few weeks followed the same pattern at the restaurant. Chuds slipped easily into the work routine and enjoyed having most of every day to work on his plans for the new venue. He took coffee most days with Ro, who seemed to be warming to him, and worked from one of the tables. He was lining up potential candidates for the units within the building and Mona had already agreed to the Shisha Lounge and VIP room. The cinema would be a club allowing them to show digital movies while offering a meal and alcoholic beverages for an inclusive price and a national chain was interested in a small e-Bingo hall.

The original idea for a video games arcade was being replaced with a tournament hall for National Champion video gamers who would stream on Twitch live while competing as well as providing terminals for the public to play on non-tournament nights and for one on one coaching sessions.

Everything was falling into place nicely, and the estate agency had drafted a contract which they had sent to Chuds for review. Once this was in place he contacted his former Solicitor, Anil.

Anil's family was one of the original Indian families to settle in Gravesend and they had lived in the same road, in fact almost opposite to each other as teenagers until he went off to University to study law. Upon his return he had set up a solicitor's practice and had helped Chuds a lot while he was setting up businesses within the town.

Almost nothing Chuds had done previously had been planned, the businesses mostly fell his way and Anil, and later with his legal partners, had helped set up small companies limiting the liability of all involved and providing a lawful appearance for enterprises that sometimes stretched the definition of lawful.

"Anil, this is Chuds Douglas, how are you my old friend?"

"Chuds! I had heard a rumour that you were back in town, it's been a long time. I expected you to contact me earlier."

"I wanted to get the lay of the land first Anil. Tell me, how's my pension plan doing?"

"To be honest I haven't checked it for a while Chuds, but I can get the figures ready within 48 hours, would that be okay with you."

"That should be fine Anil. Is there enough left to get a cashier's check for 100K ready for that meeting?"

"I'm 100% positive that's no problem Chuds, who should I make it out to?"

Chuds gave him the business name of the estate agents and agreed a time to meet.

"We moved Chuds, I'll text you the new address, we've expanded a bit."

"Fair enough Anil, and I'll try and work out what all this texting business is about."

"Smart man like you Chuds, you got it I'm sure."

"See you in 2 days Anil," Chuds disconnected the call, slipped the phone into his pocket and got ready for the evening shift at the restaurant.

It was Friday and the customer flow followed the traditional pattern of families in the early evening and the more raucous crowd drifting in later. Chuds slipped into his zen state and just focussed on washing the dishes and keeping his area clean. He heard Johnny Mowton setting up his equipment, tuning his guitar and mic checking, but just carried on dishwashing and occasionally joining in some of the staff banter.

The man who likes to be called Antonio was in fine form and his accent, now proven beyond a shadow of a doubt to be fake, was getting stranger by the minute. His stories of "The olda country" were met with, "What Chatham?" and whereas he previously might have feigned being offended, he played along and made up ridiculous tales of learning to cook "ata my sweeta Mama's knee," which again was countered with "and other low places Antonio?"

Yet through all this Chuds was constantly amazed at the efficiency of the kitchen. The time between orders and table delivery were so short, it felt almost like the man who liked to be called Antonio was psychic and knew in advance what was going to be ordered. No wonder Steve tolerated his eccentricities.

Steve walked through with a pile of plates and told Chuds that Johnny would like to talk to him.

"Send him back Steve, I can wash plates and talk at the same time."

"Proper multitasker eh? I'll send him through."

The singer pushed through the swing doors and looked at the kitchen in wonder.

"First time back here?"

"That it is Chuds, that it is. Impressive place for sure and Steve tells me you're a major asset."

"I do my best Johnny, how can I help you?"

"I heard a whisper that you might be doing something with the old Bingo Hall Chuds. Is that right?"

"Where did you hear that Johnny?" Chuds was not happy. He had taken care to try and keep all of the plans confidential, yet here was a travelling musician, who didn't even live in the town, asking about the project.

"Don't panic Chuds, Steve let slip that you might not be here much longer as you had a project in the works."

That answer didn't really satisfy as he had the feeling that Johnny knew too many details, such as the venue, for it to be just a little idle gossip from Steve. Chuds did not want the Basha family getting wind of the project until it was too late for them to do anything to try and block it, or interfere in any way. He would talk to Steve later, but for now he simply said, "Nothing definite Johnny and please keep anything you heard to yourself, I don't want to jinx anything."

"I'll be the soul of discretion Chuds, but I have an idea. Ever thought of a karaoke room?"

"To be honest Johnny, no. Is that an actual thing? I thought it was just something that popped up at pubs when they couldn't afford a real entertainer."

"Well, that does happen Chuds but it is a thing and that thing has massive potential. To be honest with you I'd be interested in running something there, maybe rent a room out for parties, one on one vocal coaching and even just public karaoke entertainment. The outlay is pretty minimal and so are the running costs."

"I'll tell you what Johnny, I'm too busy to talk about this tonight. These plates and dishes are not gonna clean themselves. Write something out for me, like a business plan, and we'll get our heads together later. Oh, and keep this quiet, you sure that nobody else told you about this?

"No Chuds, honest. Just Steve mentioned something."

Getting back to the dishes Chuds considered the idea more closely. It would certainly be something original in the area and wouldn't attract any undue attention from the law, which would be important if any of the space would eventually be used for less reputable businesses, as often seemed to happen.

There was a nagging feeling though that somebody was talking too much, he would ask Steve where he had heard about the Old Bingo Hall, because Chuds hadn't mentioned it to him.

At the end of the evening, the staff all took a thank you drink with Steve and Chuds asked him what he had heard about any plans.

"Only what Ronnie told his sister Chuds, I hope I didn't say anything out of turn."

"Hopefully not too much damage done Steve, but keep it all quiet for now. I'll have a chat with Ronnie."

He finished his drink and went upstairs to his room, he would call Ronnie in the morning.

Chapter 20

Chuds called Ronnie the next morning and arranged to meet him for a coffee at Ro's cafe. He was getting on well with Ro and she never seemed to mind him meeting business contacts and friends there, as long as he drank some coffee and didn't try and talk to her too much.

He ordered a tea for Ronnie, a coffee for himself and a couple of pieces of carrot cake. Just as she brought them to the table Ronnie arrived and let slip one of his usual greetings.

"Alright Chuds! 'Ows yer belly off for spots this morning?"

"Morning Ronnie, I got a tea for you and a bit of cake. Carrot ok?"

"Carrot tea Chuds? What the fuck did they teach you over there?"

Ronnie's grin was wide and genuine. He didn't seem to be worried that Chuds had asked to see him at short notice. After a few pleasantries were swapped and some tea and coffee sipped Chuds asked him directly if he had been talking to anyone about his plans to get back into business. Ronnie told him that he had talked to his sister and he supposed that she "might" have talked to Steve, but he assured his old friend that he hadn't talked to anyone else about it.

"Ronnie, you know you have to be careful with this info. I don't want anyone sticking a rod between the spokes of this bike, if you get my drift?"

"I think I know what you mean Chuds, sorry if I spoke out of turn. It won't happen again. How are things shaping up anyway?"

"Pretty good Ronnie, pretty good. Look you really gotta keep this to yourself but, as long as I can get the financing sorted, we are going to open 2 venues in the one building. One will be open to the public gaming, e-bingo, some high end machines and such, and at the back will be a "Gentleman's Club.""

"You ain't gonna find many Gentlemen in Gravesend any more Chuds. What kind of club?"

"You remember the old Grove Club? Good food, a lively bar and a place to relax your cares away?"

"I sure do Chuds, I spent many a weekend evening in there, and quite a few quid too, not that I remember too much about it though."

"I'm going to take it up to the next level Ronnie. There will be a limited menu, but I'll hire a good cooking crew, a well stocked bar open to members only and we'll get some ladies in to keep the guys company."

He carefully explained his plans to Ronnie, outlining how he would have VIP rooms for the guys to take their escorts back to for some privacy and intimacy, the girls would get a cut of any money spent on buying drinks for them and could negotiate their own fees inside the rooms.

Ronnie cut in a few times with some comments that he thought were witty, they weren't really, and seemed to be under the impression that he was manipulating information out of Chuds, who of course elaborated even more.

"Okay Ronnie, I gotta see someone else soon, but please keep this to yourself. Nobody needs to hear this until we're sure about the financing and the plans are under way."

"You know me Chuds, soul of discretion, Mum's the word."

Ronnie finished his tea and cake and left. Smiling Chuds walked over to the counter and asked Ro for another coffee.

"Was you serious about all that?" Ro asked him.

"Nope! Not a fucking word Ro. I just want to find out where that bit of info goes from here."

"Because if you are, I'm sure me and Mum would like to get involved."

"Ro, your Mum and I go back a long way. I wouldn't do anything like that without bringing her on board, but I was just dangling some bait there."

"Well look Chuds," this was the first time that she had ever called him Chuds and he smiled inwardly, "I'm a hard working girl, if you got anything there for me, I would love to be involved."

"Like I said Ro, it'll be through your Mum if anything happens but you'd do best to forget what you just heard 'cause not a word of it is true."

He walked back to the table and started to sip his coffee, looking out of the window and watching the world walk past. His new phone made a noise and he looked at the screen. It was a message from Anil suggesting a meeting for Monday morning, and promising to have the cashier's cheque ready for the estate agent.

Chuds agreed to the meet then just sat back in his chair and drank his coffee until it was time to walk down to the restaurant and take a nap before work. He said goodbye to Ro, who reminded him that she was open to offers.

"Just like your Mum then eh?"

"Fuck off Chuds, you know what I mean."

"I do Ro, and trust me I won't forget you."

"Whatever."

The air outside was crisp and thanks to a light breeze Chuds could smell the river from the bottom of the High Street. He really did love the River Thames, and was so happy to see it busy again. He remembered his childhood, visiting his Grandad's work site and going on the barges and lighters. He especially remembered the trips on the ferry over to Tilbury when his Grandad would take him around the old fort and stop for a pint at The World's End pub. Chuds would sit outside with a cream soda and a bag of crisps and just smell the air, while his Grandad had a couple of beers inside.

His Grandad had been a no-nonsense man. If he had a filter between his mind and his mouth, Chuds had never seen it operational. In his mind he remembered him as a big man, but having seen some old photos recently he knew this was not true. His heart though was huge, and he would help any one of his friends or neighbours, whenever he could.

Chapter 21

1960 - The day Chuds met death.

Six year old Chuds had spent the night at his grandparent's house. His dad was a shift worker and his Mum often ill, so he stayed there quite a lot.

While eating his cornflakes he could tell that his Grandmother was not her usual self. She was quieter than normal and was talking in loud whispers to his Grandad. He just got on with eating and sipping his orange squash, pretending not to notice that anything was different.

Finally his Grandfather said, "Chuds, get dressed we have a job to do."

His Grandmother replied, "George are you sure, he's just a boy."

"Julia the sooner he gets experiences like this the better, hurry up Chuds get your togs on."

Chuds finished his breakfast and ran up the stairs to get dressed. When he got back down his Grandad had his usual jacket and flat cap on and was waiting by the front door. He held his hand out and Chuds took it gladly. Whenever he walked with this man he put his small hand in that large hand and felt fully protected against anything.

"Chuds, we're only going two doors up. Mr Gilson died last night, we just have to say some nice words to his wife and close his eyes."

"You mean we're going to see a dead body Grandad?"

"Yep, nothing to be scared of Chuds, just keep your chin up, we're all heading there eventually."

His grandfather knocked on the door of number 1, and took his cap off. When the knock was answered he quietly said, "Sorry to hear about Albert Mrs G. Can we do anything for you?"

"You could close the old bastards eyes for me. I keep thinking he's looking at me, giving me the willies for sure."

"Not a problem, Come on Chuds, lets go give Albert some rest."
He could tell that Chuds was nervous and gently squeezed his hand as he led him into the front room. Albert had taken to sleeping on the sofa apparently as his health made him restless at night. His body lay there, on its side, and his eyes stared straight ahead, a little glassy. Young Chuds shuddered and his Grandad said calmly, "This happens to us all eventually Chuds, that's why it's so important to live well. I'll turn him at the shoulders, you steady his feet for me, don't worry he won't say anything."

As nervous as he was Chuds took comfort from his Grandfather's calm manner and held the dead man's feet as he was turned onto his back. Once he had settled him his Grandad put a finger on each of Albert's eyelids and pulled them closed. Then he covered him with a blanket.

Walking back out to the rear room he asked Mrs Gilson if she had told anyone yet. She said no, and so he offered to walk up to the police station with Chuds and tell them.

"Do you want to stay with Julia?" he asked her.

"No George, it's ok. I'll stay here with Albert."

Chuds Grandad led him from the house and they walked up the road to Perry Street. The Police station was a short walk up Vale Road and holding his Grandson's hand he led him across Perry Street to the front of the All Saint's Church. Sitting just outside the gate in a small wooden hut was the vicar, draped in a black cape and holding a collection box.

As they walked past the reverend he said, "Alms for the Church Mr. Douglas?"

Without even giving the vicar a glance he quietly said "Get a real fucking job," as he walked by.

Her never released his grip on his grandson's hand as they walked up to the small Police station where they reported the death of their neighbour to the duty officer. He thanked them and they watched as he dispatched a constable to ride down to the house on his bike.

Chapter 22

Chuds opened the window in his small room and laid on the bed. Taking a deep breath he could smell and feel the River at the bottom of the street, and as he drifted off into his pre-work nap he could feel his late Grandad's hand holding his.

He woke after a couple of hours and washed and changed to get ready for the Sunday evening shift, the memories of his Grandfather lingered and he felt a sense of comfort from them.

Going down to the restaurant he made himself an espresso and got his station ready for the evening's work, he chatted to the staff, swapping banter and smiles as he got everything prepared. Gradually the public started coming in and the evening couldn't have been more uneventful.

A slow and steady stream of diners, the orders arrived, were fulfilled and served, and were always followed by a pile of plates and dishes. Chuds went into his zone, blocking out almost everything around him and focussing exclusively on washing and cleaning.

At the end of the evening, as the staff left and everyone said their good nights he went up to the small room, showered and climbed into bed, where he fell asleep quickly and deeply.

The following morning he went for breakfast at Ro's, he was the first customer, and Ro herself did not seem fully awake. She knew what he wanted and he sat at the table working through the menu on his phone while he waited. Then the device gave a sound and he received the message from his solicitor, Anil, confirming their meeting and assuring him that the requested cheque was ready for collection.

After his coffee and toast Chuds said goodbye to Ro, who grunted in response, and he started his walk to the new offices of Anil Singh and Associates. The walk took around 30 minutes and as always he enjoyed looking at the town, noting the changes, appreciating the older buildings and businesses. He genuinely felt a bond with the old town, which surprised him after all of those years away.

Anil's new offices were nice. There was no other word to describe them really, they were bland and unremarkable but definitely nice. A young lady sat in reception looking at her phone, and she faced a very small switchboard, her desk top was clean and clear of junk and she smiled broadly as Chuds entered.

"Good morning. Mr Douglas?"

Chuds smiled back and said, "Mr. Douglas was my father, I'm Chuds, please use that."

"Of course Mr. Chuds. I'll tell the boss you are here."

He started to correct her but thought better of it as she had quickly picked up her desk phone, hit a button on the switchboard and already announced "Mr. Chuds here for the boss."

Looking at Chuds with a broad smile she said, "He won't keep you long, have a seat Mr. Chuds."

"It's just Chuds, no Mr."

"Oh, OK Mr Chuds, I'll remember that," and she went back to her phone screen.

Just as he was about to sit down the door to the receptionist's left opened and Anil walked into reception. He was still handsome with his trademark goatee beard, but both beard and hair were peppered with white now. He reached out a hand for Chuds to shake but when he grabbed it he pulled them together and gave Chuds a strong hug.

"Damn it is SO good to see you Chuds, you look, erm, older."

"Because I am Anil, and if you get any more white hair in that beard people will be asking you for the secret herb and spice recipe of KFC."

"Fuck you Chuds Douglas, I'm gorgeous. Come upstairs we'll catch up."

Following him up the stairs and into a long corridor they walked past several smaller offices with young men and women working on folders of papers and looking at computer screens, finally arriving at Anil's office. It was medium size, not in any way grandiose and very "nicely" furnished.

"IKEA?" Chuds said with a grin.

"Yeah, but the good IKEA Chuds," he pointed to a two seater couch for Chuds to sit on and Anil took a seat in an armchair. "You want a coffee, tea, water, a beer?"

"No, I'm all good Anil just finished breakfast. You've come up in the world."

"Hard work Chuds, there's no other secret to success, just hard work, oh and a healthy investment from my Dad."

Anil gave him a brief history of how the company had been built up before he reached into his jacket pocket and pulled out an envelope.

"Here's your cheque Chuds, 100K drawn on my business bank. There'll be a small fee for the transfer," He winked at his old friend, "nothing exorbitant mind, just to cover the expenses. No need for anyone to know where the dosh came from."

Taking the envelope Chuds slipped it into his own jacket pocket without checking it.

Anil leaned back in the armchair and crossed one leg over the other.

"Chuds I hear you're washing dishes at a High Street restaurant, is that true?"

Chuds nodded in response.

"May I ask why? Do you have any idea how much money you have available in your 'pension plan' that could be liquidated quickly if needed?"

"I haven't got a clue Anil, I know what was there when I left the country but I have no idea what's there now. I didn't even know if you were still around or if I could access it."

"If I could be bothered, I'd be offended at that Chuds," both men laughed.

Anil pulled out a folder from his messenger bag and opened it up to take out a large spreadsheet print out. He offered to go through it with Chuds, but he motioned Anil to keep it.

"Just give me the Reader's Digest Anil."

"Chuds I don't know what qualifies as wealthy nowadays, I know I don't qualify myself but you are definitely knocking at the door of being considered quite well off. Taking out the 100K sitting in your skyrocket, and estimating the fees involved in liquidating certain assets you can rest assured that you are still worth well over 700K and possibly a bit more."

"That's nice to hear Anil. Couldn't round that up to a ready million could you?"

"I could not."

Chuds eventually accepted the spreadsheet print out at his friend's insistence but didn't look at it, and would burn it as soon as he got back to the restaurant. They spent almost an hour talking about old times, old friends and what had happened to Chuds in America.

"It's not my field of expertise but I can look into getting your US ban shortened if you like."

"No need Anil, I'm not interested in going back. Look I really appreciate you looking after this money for me, have you been taking your fees?"

"Who the fuck do you think paid for this place?"

"You're welcome Anil. I'll catch up with you again very soon, going to need some contracts drawn up and a few other bits and bobs."

"We'll be proud to represent you Chuds, as always."

"Can I just ask, do you do any work for the Basha Family?"

"No chance Chuds I don't need anything badly enough to dip a toe in those waters."

"Good to hear Anil. I'll find my own way back downstairs, I'll be in touch real soon."

"Looking forward to it."

As he walked across the reception room floor the receptionist looked up from her phone and said, "Bye Mr. Chuds, it was nice to meet you." "It's just Chuds, no need for the..." but her head was already buried back in the contents of her phone screen so he simply opened the door and left.

Chapter 23

Following a pint of Guinness and a light lunch at one of the national chain pubs, he walked back down the high street and stopped in at Ro's for a pre-shift cappuccino. Sitting at his favourite window seat he pulled a small notebook out of his jacket pocket as well as the envelope with the cheque inside, he looked it over and everything was made out properly so he sent a text to the estate agent asking for a meeting on Tuesday morning.

He sipped his cappuccino and thought to himself that if Ro was as good at her other job as she was at making coffee she must be very popular with her clients. His phone pinged and the estate agent confirmed their meeting and Chuds jotted the details inside his notebook.

He looked through the notes about the new business, reading through the idea sketches that he had drawn up. He knew nothing about gaming but he had watched some Twitch streams on his phone of young men and women playing them and damn, he had gotten caught up in them and found himself cheering them on. He had realized that sports watching was just watching other people doing something they loved, so why not gaming, plus there seemed to be big money involved.

Looking over at Ro behind the counter he asked her, "Ro, you know anything about Karaoke?"

"Little bit, everyone says they won't sing, then they always do and once they start they won't stop."

"I've got a guy interested in taking some space from me for a karaoke centre, reckons it could be a good business."

"I reckon he might be right Chuds, party nights, kids and adults parties, singers looking for somewhere to practice that ain't their shower. For parties there'll be catering and drinks, I think it could be a winner and I don't know of another one in the area."

"Cheers Ro, I'm a bit excited to see his business proposal now."

"This is you excited is it? Fuck me Chuds, if you was one of my customers and you looked like that when you're excited, I'd be offering you a refund."

Chuds raised his coffee cup in a toast gesture towards his new friend and sipped his coffee some more.

"Mind if I sit here until I have to go to work Ro?"

"Keep buying coffee Chuds you can sit here all fucking night too if you want."

"Well, at least one more Ro, freshen this up for me will you?" He raised his cup towards her again. She brought him another coffee and he went back to looking through his notes, jotting down fresh ideas and making small diagrams of the layout.

After a couple of hours he packed his notebook away and bade Ro farewell as left to go back to the restaurant.

At 4 pm he went down to the kitchen and started to prep his area, greeting the staff and getting everything ready. The evening started slowly and when he put his head out into the restaurant area to say hello to Steve he noticed that the corner table was reserved again, presumably for one of the Basha family.

"This should be interesting," he said quietly.

The restaurant was quiet but Chuds zoned again, focussing entirely on his work. Just nodding politely at the staff who brought the plates through, placing the pots at their correct cooking stations, loading the plate racks. It was nice to have evenings like this after a busy weekend.

Steve came through to the kitchen around 9:00 and told Chuds that Mr Basha was in the restaurant and asking to see him.

"You want to come to the restaurant floor or shall I send him back to your 'office' Chuds?"

"I'll come out to the table Steve, if that's okay with you."

"Just keep it civil Chuds, please, I've got a good reputation in this place and I don't want to lose it."

"I won't let you down Steve."

As he walked out onto the restaurant floor he noted that there were only 2 occupied tables and they were well away from the corner table. Basha himself was sitting alone at the table and behind him stood a large man, no make that a very large man, who didn't take his eyes off of Chuds as he walked towards his boss. Chuds met his gaze and winked, which seemed to somehow piss off the bodyguard.

Chuds gestured towards a chair and said, "May I?"

Basha nodded and took a mouthful of food, which he chewed carefully and swallowed before wiping his mouth with a napkin which he laid on the table next to his plate.

"Mr Douglas," he paused, presumably for dramatic effect but before he could continue Chuds interrupted.

"I thought we'd covered this Mr Basha, just call me Chuds."

Both the bodyguard and Basha looked displeased at the interruption, it had definitely spoiled the mood that Basha was trying to create.

"As you wish... Chuds, I have heard some rumours that you are starting a new business. Would you care to discuss it with me?"

"Not really Mr Basha. I don't believe I have to report any of plans to you. Now I should be getting back to work, those dishes won't clean themselves."

"Wait Mr.. sorry Chuds, wait. I have heard that you may be planning something that might affect some of my business interests. Would you tell me about your Gentlemen's Club idea?"

"I will tell you only one thing, maybe two, but we'll start with one. There is no Gentlemen's Club planned, that was merely a scenario made up for me to determine who was telling you about my day to day activities. I will deal with Ronnie later and you need not concern yourself with that idea at all."

Basha did not look convinced, but did seem a little uneasy that Chuds had worked out who was informing on him. There could, of course, be more than one person but his gut told him it was just Ronnie running one of his side schemes.

"Okay, I will tell you a second thing Mr Basha. There is a lot of room in this town I have no idea why you are interested in anything I might want to do. Competition makes us all better, but I really don't see that I will present any kind of competition to you or your family. As a courtesy I will tell you that I am interested in renovating the old Bingo Hall, but way before you came to this town that used to be a magnificent cinema. It was where I watched my first ever movie, sitting in velvet seats, licking my Choc Ice, and enthralled by the hidden luxury in this grimy town. I want to renovate it back to that former glory and put some modern business in there related to the entertainment field."

Chuds poured himself a glass of water from the pitcher on the table and took a sip. While he looked at Basha he kept an eye on the big man in his peripheral vision. Placing the glass back on the table he continued.

"You may have heard stories about me from the past Mr Basha, some of them may even be true but I assure that they have been embellished in my absence. I have no desire to do anything other than refurbish a childhood memory and create something nice for the public. I will not inform you of my plans unless you're on the local planning committee. I'm just a business man trying to get a fresh start."

Basha took another bite of his food and looked at Chuds for a long time.

"I want to believe you, I really do. However you worry me Chuds, and I don't like to worry. I'm going to keep my eyes on you."

"Well, some people say it's a free country. They're wrong of course, but you know, you have to spend your time as you see fit. I assure you that if you spend time watching me you'll get very bored. Now, unless there's anything else I need to get back to my job."

Without waiting for an answer Chuds stood, left the table and went back to the kitchen. Steve followed him through to make sure everything was okay and expressed some concern that things might get out of control.

"I can't stop that happening, but if you like Steve I can move out and quit the job. I don't want to but I also don't want anything I'm doing to impact your business.

"I don't want to lose you from the kitchen Chuds but I also know you're way too good for that job. Maybe if you just found somewhere else to live, then these meetings don't have to take place in here."
"Gotcha Steve, I've got plans up in the smoke tomorrow but I'll look for a place as quickly as I can after that."

"Maybe Ronnie knows somewhere for you to rent Chuds."

"Steve I'm pretty sure Ronnie won't be doing me any favours in the future. Don't worry, I'll find somewhere as quickly as I can."

Chapter 24

The next morning, as he rode the train to London, Chuds called Anil to see if he knew anywhere that he could rent a couple of rooms or a studio apartment. It was time to get an office area that was a little less public than Ro's Coffee shop and a place to live that would separate him from the restaurant job. Anil promised to look around and let him know.

Chuds closed his eyes and wondered what to do about Wrong Way Ronnie. They had been friends a very long time and it hurt that he had sold out to Basha, but there was no contract between them. It was obvious though that he couldn't trust him any more. He would have a word with him tomorrow. He sent him a text that invited him for a lunch and a pint at Poncy Pete's pub, and promised no trouble, just clear the air.

Then he relaxed until the train pulled into Waterloo East Station. Making the short walk to the offices of the Estate Agent, Chuds took in the surroundings. He always looked up to find the real London but also enjoyed seeing the new businesses that continued to sprout up everywhere. The Agent was very keen to know what kind of business would be in the property and Chuda gave him a brief description of the business plan.

"It's very important to me that the exterior goes back as close to the original Regal Cinema appearance as possible and that will carry through into the reception area, which will resemble the foyer of the cinema as well. There will be several small business entertainment outlets inside of the building including a cinema club, an e-gaming auditorium, a karaoke area and a relaxation lounge. Nothing definite yet, but we have advanced plans and we'll move on them as soon as possible."

"This all sounds marvellous," the agent seemed genuinely interested, "I will definitely come to visit once you are open."

"That's great, call me before you come, I'll give you the VIP tour," and Chuds took the folder of papers, shook the agent's hand and left the offices.

He decided to find a small cafe or restaurant for lunch and walked around the local area looking for an appealing spot. Settling on a small Greek restaurant Chuds ordered a Greek Salad and a glass of white wine. While enjoying the fresh food he received a message from Anil offering him the chance to look at a 2 bedroom flat on the riverfront and a separate message from Ronnie agreeing to meet the next day for lunch.

The riverfront apartment sounded ideal and he asked his solicitor if he could see it that afternoon, which apparently was okay so he confirmed 6:00 as an appointment time. This would work out well, he could take the train back to Gravesend, walk down to Ro's for a coffee then on down the High Street to check out the flat. The thought of living on the river was very appealing and he hoped that the apartment was nice.

He was not disappointed.

On his way to see the apartment he had stopped for a coffee and mentioned to Ro that he wouldn't be working from her cafe any more if the apartment was suitable.

"Oh that'll be a loss," she replied sarcastically, but Chuds had a feeling that she would miss him.

The apartment turned out to be really nice. The living room area looked out over the river and the smaller bedroom would make a nice office. He asked Anil to rent it through one of the companies and agreed to take residence the next day. The furniture that was there would do for now and he would convert the small bedroom later. As Anil shook his hand and agreed to handle the deal (for that small fee of course) he kept hold of Chuds' hand and asked him something interesting yet also slightly worrying.

"Chuds, why did you ask me about the Basha family?"

"Oh, I've had a couple of run-ins with the Dad and a small scuffle with one of the sons, I just don't want crossed wires or mixed business interests Anil."

"Well one of the sons, some plonker called 'Bash' Basha, who was really full of himself came to the offices yesterday. Wanted to know if we'd represent them in some acquisitions, which I politely declined as I have full case loads at the moment."

"I appreciate that Anil, but I really don't want to cost you any income, you could take their work if you like."

"Not a fucking chance Chuds, I'd like to tell you that it's because of our undying love for you and respect for our long business association, but honestly they scare the shit out of me."
"I never knew you was that sensitive Anil, you old softy. I appreciate it and that fear is I think healthy."

Anil handed Chuds the keys and told him he could take possession at noon the next day. He decided to celebrate by walking along to Poncy Pete's for a pint and some good company. Fat Mona was behind the bar and she squealed when she saw his reflection in the bar mirror, then a higher pitched squeal came from upstairs before Pete ran down and planted a kiss on his cheek.

"First pint is on the house Chuds."

"What if I'm only having one?"

"Then it's a free one you silly cow!"

"Cheers Pete, how's business?"

"Mid week, it's usually quiet Chuds, thank God that Mona and I have a few other irons in the fire," and he winked overtly.

Chuds told them about the apartment that he was taking just down the road and mentioned that he had started solid plans to open a small entertainment complex. He urged them to keep all details secret until he was ready to go public.

"Mona I want to make a relaxation area, themed, members only that would enable you to run a very discrete place there. The problem is we have to be seen NOT to encroach on the Basha's business interests, at least in the short term."

"Chuds. Those toe rags deal in underage girls and most of them are drugged and trafficked. How they've not been shut down and arrested I have no idea. We can have a lounge area, nice music, upscale snacks and some private rooms. I think we can avoid any conflict."

"Speaking of conflict," Chuds interjected, "I'm meeting Ronnie here tomorrow for lunch. He's been informing on my activities to the Basha family, I need to straighten things out with him."

Pete looked genuinely sad, decided a second round of drinks was in order and started pulling pints. The three friends enjoyed an evening of reliving old friendships, catching Chuds up on information about old colleagues and swapping old stories. At about 11:00 he left the pub, planting a kiss on Mona and Poncy Pete's cheeks and walked up to the restaurant.

He checked through the front windows that Basha's table was unoccupied and went in through the front door. Steve was behind the bar and he told him about the apartment but offered to keep working as a dishwasher for as long as he was needed.

Steve seemed relieved that Chuds was moving out but asked him to stay on on the kitchen for as long as he wanted.

"Thanks Steve, I appreciate all that you've done for me. By the way could you give me the phone number for Johnny Mowton?"

"I can, but you're not gonna steal my singer are you?"

"Wouldn't dream of it Steve but I want to run a couple of ideas by him."

Chapter 25

The next morning Chuds packed his clothes into a rucksack, told the lunch crew that he was moving out but would be back for the evening shift and walked down to Pete's pub. He dropped his bag behind the bar and waited for Ronnie to show up.

Eventually a text came from Ronnie's phone saying he was not going to make the meeting. Chuds called back on the number and it rang for a long time before being answered by a female voice. He explained that he had a meeting arranged with the owner of the phone and was calling to see if everything was okay.

"Sir, this is Darent Valley Hospital, your friend is undergoing some procedures, I will ask him to contact you later," and the phone disconnected quickly.

Chuds called Pete over to ask him if he had heard anything, but he had no idea what could have happened, so Chuds asked him to call a taxi to take him to the hospital.

When he arrived he was told that Ronnie was resting in a ward room and Chuds asked to see him. Despite it not being visiting hours they allowed him to go to the ward and he was shocked to see a policeman sitting by Ronnie's bed.

Ronnie was laying down, his face heavily bandaged but Chuds could see the cuts and bruises underneath and an eyepatch covered his left eye. The policeman looked at Chuds suspiciously, he also looked to be about 12 years old to Chuds, which did not fill him with confidence.

"Can I talk to him?"

Before the cop could answer Ronnie groaned and said, "Yeah you can talk to me Chuds."

"What happened Ronnie."

"Bash Basha happened Chuds. But you should see what I did to him. I fucked his fists right up. With my face."

"Why Ronnie, why did he do this?"

"Said I caused his Dad to be embarrassed by getting caught out ratting on you. I figured you'd be the one to give me a spanking Chuds, not that ape."

"You know I wouldn't lay a finger on you Ronnie. I was disappointed that you reported on me to them, but I've known you a long time. I doubt we will do business again Ronnie but I'd never have done something like this."

"Well he offered money Chuds and you didn't."

"Dish washing doesn't pay enough to hire staff Ronnie, but you know I would have looked after you in time."

"In time don't pay the bills Chuds. I'm sorry, I really am."

"Don't worry about it Ronnie, and I'll cover any bills you run up in here. I'll take care of this."

As he stood to leave the young policeman also stood and started to say something, but Chuds shut him down. He called for a taxi and rode back to Pete's pub to collect his bag and tell them what had happened.

Both Mona and Pete were horrified to hear what the news. Chuds grabbed his bag and walked down to his new apartment. Once there he called Steve at the restaurant and explained that he would be late in.

"About that Chuds. Look Ronnie is family and this beating resulted from you talking to Basha senior in my restaurant. It's too close to home Chuds. I'm going to have to let you go. I can't have shit like this anywhere near the business."

"I understand Steve. Honestly it's all okay. I took my stuff from the room and I'll drop the keys off later."

"Thanks for being a sport Chuds, I wish you well."

"You too Steve."

Chuds stood by the large living room window and looked out at the river. He remembered something his Grandad had told him.

"When one door closes, open it again because that's how doors work."

He guessed that he was going to be watched for a while so he took a collapsible baton from his bag and put it in his jacket pocket, then walked up the High Street. He dropped the keys off at the restaurant, shook Steve's hand and carried on walking up to the top of the High Street. Sitting on one of the bench seats he took out his phone and scrolled through some news items. Finally he saw the big guy who had been at the restaurant with Basha Senior watching him. Making eye contact he motioned for him to come over to the metal bench and indicated that he should take a seat.

"How's your English?"

"Probably better than yours, I was born in London."

Chuds looked at him and smiled. "Tell me what happened to my friend Ronnie."

"Look, that was all Basha, trying to act big. His dad had no idea he would do that, but he just goes mental sometimes."

"How will his Dad react if I do an eye for an eye? You know I can't just let it go."

"He'd be angry but probably would just call for a meeting with you. I would have to try and stop you of course, but I wouldn't try too hard, if you know what I mean."

"I'm going to walk down to the Gordon Gardens and enjoy some time sitting by the river. Maybe Basha will join me?"

"You never know."

Chuds stood to walk away and the big man pulled out a phone and sent a message. It was getting dark as he walked onto the promenade area. He found a bench seat facing the river and sat, and waited. Within an hour he saw the big guy and Bash Basha walking towards him. He placed a hand on the baton inside his jacket and let them both get close. Bash walked with a swagger, but Chuds knew from experience that he couldn't really back it up. The big man though seemed like he knew what he was doing.

They approached Chuds who stayed seated and Bash came WAY too close thinking he would intimidate Chuds by leaning over him.

"Did you like what I did to your little rat friend?"

"Oh, that was you?"

"Yeah it was me and I'm about to give you some of the same, nobody embarrasses my family and gets away with it."

"Funny that because I get the idea that you embarrass them all the fucking time."

"What did you just say to me?"

Chuds saw that the big guy took a step back, he bought out the baton, flicked it to full extension and in one move brought it from the left side of his body and slammed it into Basha's kneecap. Basha fell to the ground and Chuds quickly stood and stamped hard on the same knee.

Looking at the big guy he mouthed "Sorry about this" and slammed the baton into his throat. The big guy gulped hard as he tried to breathe before falling to his knees and Chuds placed a kick onto the side of his head driving him to the ground.

Turning back to Bash he saw that he was clutching at his knee and staring at Chuds with pure hatred.

"Look you little shit, I could take you out right here and just roll you into the fucking river. But honestly I have a mix of respect and pity for your dad."

Chuds kicked Bash in the ribs a few times, feeling one of them crack then he stomped hard onto his cheek, driving his face into the gravel. He ground the helpless man's face into the pavement to inflict damage that would look a lot worse than it was.

Leaning down to Bash's ear he whispered, "I'm letting you off easy, but if you come near me or my friends again I will finish this job properly, understand?"

Without waiting for a reply he stood up straight and walked over to the big man, who was clutching his throat and finally managing to get some air. Looking back at Bash on the ground he placed a kick into the big man's stomach, but pulled it short. You'd never know from the grunt that he let out though.

"And if you're ever going to bring muscle, bring someone bigger."

He winked at the big guy and mouthed the word "Sorry".

As he walked away he collapsed the baton and dropped it into a drain, then walked to a different pub for a Guinness, no sense dragging any trouble that might follow into Pete's place.

Chapter 26

Chuds sat at the pub's bar, sipping a cool draught Guinness and as the adrenaline wore down he started to feel tired. Undoubtedly there would be repercussions from Basha Senior but there was no sense worrying about that until tomorrow. From his wallet he pulled the business card that Marti had given him when she gave him a lift, he thought it would be nice to have dinner with her tomorrow and find out what was going on in her life.

When she answered the phone they chatted for a little while, it felt very easy to talk to her and he asked if she would like to have dinner the next evening at the Indian Restaurant adjoining his new apartment. She agreed and they decided to meet there at 8:00 pm.

Then he called Ronnie's sister to see if they needed anything and she told him Ronnie would be coming home the next day but would still need bed rest.

"I'll send a care package tomorrow, and a few quid for expenses, I'm so sorry that this happened."

Then he returned to his beer but by 10:30 pm had gone back to the new flat and was already in bed.

Chuds' custom was to wake early, it was a lifelong habit and he enjoyed the sunrise in particular. Sitting at his window that overlooked the river, with the window wide open he sipped a coffee and thought back over the events of last night. He tried to decide whether he should pre-empt Basha's reaction and make contact first or just wait to see what developed. Deciding on the latter he finished his coffee, ate some toast, then contacted Anil to discuss the lease he had just signed.

Anil invited him to the offices at 11:00 am and with time to spare he showered, dressed and walked up to Ro's place for another coffee.

When he entered the cafe Ro gave him a look that was even more unwelcoming than usual.

"Something wrong Ro?"

"I heard about last night Chuds, I can't have trouble in here."

"I won't let that happen Ro,"

"Well that prick did deserve what he got, but if anything kicks off in here Chuds I'm calling the Bill straight away."

"Fair enough Ro, cappuccino?"

She brought his coffee over and he sat at the window, people watching. Then he saw Basha Senior and the big man from last night coming to the door.

As they walked in Ro said, "I've got 99 punched in already, I don't care who you are but if you start shit in here I'm hitting the other 9 and turning on the CCTV."

Basha looked at her and smiled, assured her that he just wanted to talk to Mr. Douglas here and told the big man to stay outside the door.

"Chuds. Still okay that I call you that?" Chuds nodded, "I need to ask you about last night."

"I expected that you would."

"First let me say I am sorry about your friend, that was not authorized by me, my son is rash sometimes, and after what happened by the roadside that day I am surprised that he would approach you again."

"He did a lot of damage to Ronnie for something that was not really his fault. He wasn't working for me, in fact NOBODY is working for me, but he is an old friend and I couldn't let that go."

"I understand and your loyalty to a friend that was informing on you is admirable. I suppose."

"You do know I took it easy on him, right?"

"If I hadn't seen the bruises on that man at the door, I would have thought it was a set up, but I appreciate you not doing too much damage."

"If this happens again I won't be so nice, you know that too right?"

"It won't happen again. My son is going to Albania to look after one of my business interests there for a while, I cannot have such a loose cannon running around. Chuds, can we call this 'done' and get on with our lives?"

Chuds looked over at Ro who was looking really nervous, "Mr Basha can I buy you a tea or a coffee?"

"Can that girl make espresso?"

"Best in town. Ro a double espresso and a glass of water for Mr Basha here."

Ro pulled the double shot and Chuds walked over to the counter to fetch it, he winked at Ro and she visibly relaxed.

Putting the small cup and the glass in front of Basha, he sat down and looked across the table.

"Mr Basha, to save you having me followed or putting any of my friends at risk I am going to tell you something out of courtesy. The old Bingo Hall was once the Regal Cinema, a grand building that has sentimental value to me and I have just leased it. I intend to turn it into a small entertainment complex that will include a cinema, a video gaming arena and a karaoke centre. I don't think that you are involved in any of those businesses and so I don't see that I am presenting any competition to you."

Basha nodded in agreement.

"I want you to understand that I don't feel obligated to tell you this, I am merely trying to put your mind at rest and save us all unnecessary aggravation."

"That is kind of you Mr Chuds. However, in case you think I am going soft, I will be watching your business closely."

"It's your time and your life Mr Basha."

Basha got up from the table and placed his cup on the counter in front of Ro.

"That was a good coffee my dear, I appreciate it?"

Ro picked the cup up and as she turned said quietly, "Ta."

After he had left Ro watched as Chuds slipped the large knife that had been sitting on his lap back into the inside pocket of his jacket.

"He's not so bad once you get to know him is he?" said Chuds.

"Gives me the fucking willies, and not in a good way," Ro replied.

"Ro, I hope that wasn't too bad for you, I gotta go now and see a man about a dog."

Ro turned to wash the cups and said, "Missing you already."

Chuds left and walked to Anil's offices where he met with the lawyer and handed over the large folder with the lease and associated paperwork.

"Can you recommend a property manager Anil? Or is there one of your crew that can handle a few things for me?"

"Firstly Chuds, I have associates not a fucking crew. Secondly, of course I can assign it, I have a young lady in mind." He picked up the internal phone and asked the girl on the desk to send someone called Deepa in.

Shortly after that an immaculately dressed and extremely business-like looking lady entered the office. She was probably in her late-thirties, wearing tasteful make up but with a definite Indian edge and she walked over and shook Chud's hand, firmly.

"Mr Douglas, good to see you," she paused and continued to hold his hand with a firm grip, "again."

"Again?"

"I used to work at one of your spa establishments back in the day. It paid for my law degree and even though we hardly ever saw you all the girls thought you were the bees knees. We were heartbroken when you left the country. It's really good to see you again."

"Wow, you seem to have done well for yourself, I hope the old days haven't left any scars. You fancy running a building for me, handling the renovations, getting insurances, hiring contractors ad so on?"

Deepa looked over at Anil, who nodded, and replied, "It will be my pleasure Mr Douglas."

"Please, just Chuds. Anil will give you my mobile number, consider yourself hired."

"Thanks Chuds, looking forward to helping you with this."

"Just one thing, you know that old attorney-client privilege thing? It applies double here, nothing should be leaked to anyone, Okay?"

"Not a problem Chuds, I'll send you a text so you have my number," and she turned and walked out of the room.

Leaving Anil's office Chuds walked down to the supermarket and bought a case of beer and a huge basket of fruit which he took to Ronnie's sister's house. Ronnie was home and laying on the sofa looking no better than he did the day before.

"Chuds, a little birdie told me what you did to Bash Basha, I appreciate it but I hope you haven't brought a cart load of trouble on yourself."

"It's all good and sorted Ronnie, I've already spoken to his Dad, nothing more will happen. How are you feeling?"

"Like twice hammered crap to be honest Chuds. I've got 2 cracked ribs, it hurts if I cough, if I laugh, even if I fart."

"Makes a change from your farts hurting other people Ronnie."

"Don't make me laugh Chuds, it really fucking hurts."

Chuds pulled out 200 hundred pounds and stuck it in the case of beer, which he pushed closer to the sofa. Ronnie looked up at his old friend and seemed about to cry.

"I've fucked it all up ain't I Chuds? You're never gonna hire me again are you?"

"Too soon to say Ronnie, much too soon. Look you're the best fixer I know, I've never known anyone that could source talent or artefacts quicker or better than you. Maybe in the future we can work something out, but you gotta concentrate on getting yourself better."

"It's just gonna take time Chuds, that fucker did me over well good, it's gonna take time to get back to my natural beauty. I don't wanna end up some sideshow freak, looking like the elephant man's handsome brother."

"If you don't get your looks back maybe we can bill you as the world's tallest midget, or the loudest mute, shortest giant.."

"Don't make me laugh Chuds, it fucking hurts, I swear it hurts so much."

"Just get better soon Ronnie, we'll talk when you're a bit better. If you need anything get Steve to give me a ring."

"Thanks Chuds, you're a mate."

He genuinely felt sorry for Ronnie, even though he had been wrong to spy on him for the Bashas he really didn't deserve to be hurting that badly. Chuds decided to find something for him at the new business, just not one that included any trade secrets.

Leaving the house he decided to go to his flat, take a short nap then get ready for dinner with Marti.

Chapter 27

The Ghandi Indian Restaurant was just at the end of his building. It had once been a pub and like so many pubs over the years it had closed and been repurposed. Chuds had never eaten there but he'd asked around and it was recommended so he had booked a table for 8:00 pm.

That meant that, in Chuds' world, you arrived at 7:55, which he did and he entered the restaurant, looking around to assess the place. There were only 3 other tables in use so he chose one in a corner and asked the waiter if he could wait for his friend.

Fashionably late by about 15 minutes Marti entered the restaurant and Chuds got his first good look at his old band mate. In her mid-fifties, she looked stunning, even though he had known her as a man before, it took no effort to see her as a woman now.

She was wearing a fashionable dress, her hair and make up were subtle but impressive and she looked beautiful. She walked across the room with a confident stride, smiling and as she reached Chuds she leaned in and kissed his cheek.

"Chuds, it is SO lovely to see you."

Chuds walked around and pulled her chair out for her to sit as he said, "Same here Marti, same here."

The waiter brought over two menus and poured them a glass of water each, they both ordered a glass of red wine and read the menus in silence. Finally Marti placed the menu on the table and stared at Chuds before smiling and saying, "Chuds, you're dealing with this transformation better than any one of my old friends, some of whom don't even talk to me now."

"I won't say it's not a shock Marti, but you look so good, so happy I don't know how anyone could not want this for you."

"Well, you know... some people Chuds," she left the sentence unfinished as the waiter came back and took their orders.

The waiter arrived with some poppadums and dip and as he walked away Chuds looked at Marti apologetically.

"Oh what's THAT look for Chuds?"

"Marti, I just want to say sorry for how things went down all those years ago. We were not sophisticated men and we treated you pretty badly at the end of that gig."

"Oh Chuds you don't need to apologize. Consider it as shock therapy. It was probably one of the best things that ever happened to me in the long run. Yes I was upset, I was drama queen, clutch the pearls, stomp out of the room upset, but it was what I needed, honestly."

She adjusted her hair slightly and wiped her mouth with a napkin.

"That was really the push I needed to openly admit that I was gay and I went to my parent's place on the Isle of Sheppey. After I came out to them, which went a lot better than I expected I should add, I spent a few months deciding who I really was and who I really wanted to be. It became more and more obvious to me that I wasn't just gay, I was really a woman, just shut up in the wrong body."

Chuds looked at her with absorbed interest, "Marti you never really did pull off that whole Freddie Mercury look, but I can't ever remember seeing you without a scrubby beard and your chest was hairier than a baboon's bum."

"Oh it's still hairy Chuds."

His jaw dropped as he said, "Really?"

"Of course not you fuckwit! Damn you look like a dog that's been shown a magic trick! I had everything lasered off. Oh your face Chuds, it's a fucking picture."

"Marti, I'm so far out of my field of expertise and my comfort zone here, you're gonna have to help me out."

"Now why would I do that when messing with you is so much fun?" and she giggled.

Their food arrived and the waiter placed the dishes, prepared their plates and poured the wine. They started eating and Chuds suddenly realized he was incredibly comfortable in her company.

"Tell me more about what happened when you worked out that you were really a woman, Marti. How did that all go down?"

"Do you remember meeting my Mum one time?" Chuds nodded, "She was an X-Ray tech at Minster Hospital. She fixed me up with a therapist there who kind of guided me through the whole process. It had it's ups and downs Chuds, I won't lie. I hear people now on social media belittling trans people and it makes me mad as hell. This isn't something you do on a whim and I can't imagine having gone through this without professional and family help and support."

Chuds ate a few more mouthfuls of food, even the silences here were comfortable, then he asked, "How about your voice, it's higher than I remember, even when you're just talking. I mean you're not Kate Bush, only dogs can hear you high, but you don't have that old baritone that I remember."

"I had estrogen and progestin therapy for a while, but I was worried about spoiling my voice. Singing means so much to me and I didn't want to risk ruining it. Honestly it just seemed to find a comfortable pitch after a while. There was a lot of guidance, soul searching and support Chuds."

They both carried on eating their food and sipping wine, "The hormones did a lot to feminize my body, and I had breast enhancement surgery but it was also about being comfortable with the new me."

"Well Marti, you look great and I never saw you looking this happy as Martin for sure."

"Chuds, you've got that look, I've seen it before, go on ask me?"

For the first time all evening Chuds felt really uncomfortable.

"Chuds, you want to know how far I went with the surgery don't you? Yes I still have a dick if that's what you're worried about."

"I wouldn't say worried Marti, more curious."

"It's okay, most people who find out about my past wonder also."

Chuds finished his meal, as did Marti, and they both ordered a coffee.

"Marti, I want to ask you something else, business related."

"Oh, now I'm intrigued."

He explained about the new entertainment complex and the planned renovation of the old Bingo Hall property. Describing the idea of a karaoke venue he asked if Marti would be interested in fronting it. He went through the ideas of parties, themed karaoke rooms, professional coaching and all of the possible revenue streams, explaining that the module would be operated independently by Johnny but would need a spokesperson who could sing, coach and manage the day to day.

"I'm definitely interested Chuds, subject to fine details, but I have to say, this all sounds a bit vanilla for the Chuds I used to know."

"I'm not going to lie Marti, there will probably be a bit of business there that will be 'semi legal' so to speak, but not in your section and that's one of the reasons that each entertainment module will be run by a different company."

"Oh, that's disappointing, I could do with a bit of spice in my life, I'm definitely interested Chuds, get back with me closer to the opening dates. Now are you going to take me to your flat and have wild monkey sex with me?"

"I hadn't considered it at all Marti."

"Good 'cause that would have been too awkward." She threw her head back and laughed so loud that the waiter came over to see if everything was okay.

"And then the waiter came! Fucking hell Marti, this has been a great night."

"It really has Chuds, keep me posted on the karaoke idea."

"Will do Marti, drive safe."

Chapter 28

Not having to work around the dishwashing schedule seemed to give him a lot more flexibility with his time. However, despite having allocated one bedroom as an office it still had a bed in there. so he walked up to Ro's the next morning to do some calling, texting and planning.

Ro seemed as thrilled to see him as usual, which meant not at all, and nodded at him silently as he took his regular seat. Without prompting she took him his normal toast and coffee while Chuds scribbled in his notebook.

There had been a text from Deepa to send him her number, so he texted back and asked her to arrange new locks on all doors of the property and to arrange full insurance effective as soon as possible. She responded with a thumbs up.

He called Brian and asked if they could meet for lunch at Pete's Pub and to see if he could find any archive pictures of the old Regal Cinema's frontage and foyer. Brian said he'd do his best and he agreed to meet Chuds at 1:00 pm. Just like that most of his day was covered.

He looked over at Ro, who as usual had her nose buried in her phone.

"Hey Ro, if I buy a small laptop could you help me set it up and show me how to use it, so I can order stuff for my new place?"

"I could, but I won't for free, I'm not a fucking charity worker you know."

"Oh you know I'll take care of you Ro. What should I get?"

"Apple or Windows Chuds, which do you like?"

"The easiest one of those to use Ro."
"Windows it is then," she wrote something down on a piece of paper and told him to go to Bluewater and get what she'd suggested.

"I'll go after lunch, can I book you for a quick lesson in the morning?"

"Fuck me, the things I do for friends of my Mum. Ok then."

Just after 12:00 noon Chuds walked down to Pete's pub and settled in at a small table. Fat Mona brought him a pint and he said he'd wait for Brian before ordering some food. Brian arrived suitably early and Chuds was so happy to see that he looked a lot more vital than he had before.

As Brian sat at the table Chuds noticed he now had an earring, a small gold hoop in his right ear.

"Notice anything new Chuds?"

"You mean the earring?"

"That would be it, what do you think?"

"Brian I'm not a fan, but you have to do what's good for you. I always thought only poofs, pirates and pikeys wore earrings."

"Oh, put me down for a pirate then Chuds!"

He reached into a small bag he was carrying and pulled out some papers. "These are just printed off my computer Chuds, but they're pictures of the old cinema inside and out," and he handed them across the table.

"Chuds are you okay? I heard you had a barney with that lunatic Bash Basha?"

"Let's just say he underestimated me Brian, I'm fine and I suppose you heard about Ronnie?"

"Yeah, sorry I didn't pick up that he was grassing on you Chuds."

"It's all okay Bri, we'll work through it. By the way, I'm leasing this building as of yesterday."

Brian looked stunned, "Where did you get the money for the deposit?"

"Some old friends want to invest Bri, the less you know the better.

This building looks so short and small in some of these photos."

"Well sometimes it had sort of a gantry type sign on the top saying 'Regal' but that went away over time. The exterior is still sound though Chuds, bit of renovation we can get it back to it's old glory days and inside we can get the foyer looking spick and span again"
"And if I remember it's like a TARDIS inside, goes back forever. We need to do a site inspection Brian, but I need to know that you're on board. I want you to be my manager there."

Brian smiled and said, "Of course Chuds, I'd be proud of that, and thanks for taking a chance on me, I was right down for a while there, but this project has lit my spark again, so to speak."

"Brian, a girl that works for Anil, her name is Deepa, is going to be the property manager, with all that entails. I want you to manage the day to day and coordinate the businesses."

"Businesses Chuds?"

"There's going to be a company that owns the building and the concept Bri, Anil is working on setting that up now. Then there will be modular businesses inside the venue. So far I'm working on an e-gaming arena, a karaoke venue, a Shisha and relaxation area and a film club. Each module will be operated by its own Limited Liability Company and funded by investment from the operators."

"Holy crap, you've thought this through huh?"

"Easy to do when you're washing dishes Brian."

Lunch arrived, some of Poncy Pete's finest sandwiches and Mona refreshed their beers.

"I want to run the film club myself Brian, you know it's a passion of mine. I've got a couple of young guys who are good at playing 'Call of Doody' or something like that who want to run the e-arena, do you know how much those guys can earn? Fat Mona will run the Shisha bar and lounge and Johnny from the restaurant will operate the karaoke module, but it will be fronted by Marti."

"Our Marti? Used to be Martin. Marti?"

"Yep, I had dinner with her last night, she'll be perfect. She's classy, mature and sings like an angel. She'll offer vocal coaching and arrange parties for kids and adults who want to sing their hearts out and have fun."

Brian ate some more of his sandwich and sipped his beer. He had a thoughtful expression on his face. Finally he said, "I like it Chuds, you gonna have a bar in there?"

"Drinks will be available, but my idea is from a central concession. I don't want people standing or sitting at the bar and I don't want them getting too drunk. I need to think of someone who could run that I guess."

From behind the bar someone let out a squeal.

"Of course it's you Pete, you don't think I'd offer it to anyone else do you?"

"I'm in Chuds, oh I'm all in!"

Mona walked back over to the table to give it a wipe. "Chuds, I heard about Ronnie, and what you did, that was good of you."

"Had to be done Mona, but I thought you didn't care much for Ronnie."

"He's a bit of a weasel Chuds, but I don't wish a beating like that on anyone, although I nearly gave him one myself once."

Brian looked up, "Oh do tell Mona, let's hear it."

"Nothing too serious, and it was a long time ago. Remember that little motorbike he had? He was riding it down the High Street, back when you could do that, and I was walking up to the cafe. Little bastard was coming straight at me and I thought he was going to run me down Chuds."

She paused for dramatic effect.

"He slammed his brakes on and stopped inches from my lady bits. He could have ruined my career right then, who wants to rent a fanny with tyre marks? Do you know what he said when I asked him why he didn't go round me?"

Both men shook their heads.

"Little prick said he didn't have enough petrol."

Brian snorted beer from his nose and Chuds started to choke on his sandwich.

"I can see why that would upset you Mona."

"Still I wouldn't wish that beating on my worst enemy, thanks for sticking up for him Chuds."

Glasses were raised in a toast to Ronnie.

Chapter 29

Chuds rode the bus to Bluewater in search of a laptop, and during the journey he received a text from Anil. Apparently Chuds now owned 'Regal Modular Entertainment Ltd.' and 'The Regal Film Club Ltd.' and Anil said he was waiting for input regarding the other names.

Deepa also sent him a text asking for a meeting regarding the interior plans for the new complex, and he arranged to meet her on the site the next afternoon. He was beginning to like this texting, it saved time and seemed to be very efficient.

Once at the mall, which was the biggest that he had ever seen, he found his way to the electronics shop and simply showed the salesman the note that Ro had given him. The salesman, of course, tried to up-sell him but Chuds carefully explained that he didn't dare deviate from the instructions, and that if the salesman had ever met the lady that wrote the instructions, he wouldn't be suggesting this either.

He paid for the laptop with a debit card drawn on the business bank account that Anil had set up for him, and took the bus back home. He walked up to the Cafe and gave the bags to Ro, along with 50 pounds, and asked her to set it up for him. She grunted, accepted the bags and said, "So you having a coffee or what?"

"Of course Ro, I'll just sit over here."

While sitting at the table, sipping his cappuccino he saw the big minder that had been with Bash Basha just outside. He nodded at Chuds and made a motion suggesting that he wanted to come in, so Chuds nodded in reply.

Ro tensed behind the counter, but carried on looking at her phone.

The big man entered the room and sat opposite Chuds. "Look Mr Douglas, you seem like a fair guy to me, and you held back a lot, not sure if I could have stopped you the other night even if I was trying."

"Nice of you to say so, how's the neck?"

"Oh it's okay now, listen I shouldn't really be seen in here talking to you, so I am going to suggest that you throw me out when I've finished here."

Chuds nodded.

"Basha is still watching you. He said it was all good, but he's looking for any reason to take you out. Just wanted to let you know that you should be careful."

"I always try to be careful, but I appreciate the tip off, I really do. I'm going to walk you to the door now, is that okay?"

Chuds stood and grabbed the big guy's ear pulling him roughly to his feet, twisting it slightly, enough to make his new friend wince hard, he walked him to the door, pulled it open, and with a well placed kick in the middle of the back, pushed him out of the cafe.

"Now fuck off," he yelled and closed the door hard.

"Another coffee Ro, this business stuff is making me thirsty."

"Chuds, you want me to come down to your place when I close and set this up? I need a night off my other job."

"Sure Ro, if you don't mind," and he wrote the address and flat number on a napkin and passed it over to her.

That evening she turned up carrying a McDonalds take out bag, and she ran through setting up the laptop with him while they ate cheeseburgers and fries. Chuds opened some wine and poured a couple of glasses and paid attention while Ro taught him the fundamentals of online searching, communication and shopping. He took her through and showed her the small bedroom that he wanted to make into an office and after a quick look Ro went back to the laptop, logged on to the IKEA site and ordered him a desk, office chair and a couple of filing cabinets.

"Should all be here in a couple of days Chuds, better get rid of that bed in there, want me to send someone to pick it up?"

"Sure Ro, and thanks a million for doing all this. How much do I owe you?"

"You already gave me 50 Chuds, you're all good."

He gave her another 50 anyway and asked if she needed a taxi home.

The next morning he called Brian and asked him to come over. He wanted to go through some interior layout ideas for the building, and then suggested that they both meet with Deepa in the afternoon, on site.

When Brian arrived it was just like looking at the old Brian, this project had definitely revitalised him and you could almost feel him buzzing with energy. Chuds pulled out his notebook and started to walk him through several ideas that had for the interior.

"Bri, I want to keep this as cashless inside as possible. I want an entrance booth in the foyer like there used to be at the cinema, people will buy access to whichever module they want to visit and pay there, as well as loading some kind of card that they can use to pay for drinks, snacks and any extras. Well, most extras, some will have to be cash of course."

Brian nodded his agreement.

"The old circle seating, I want that to be the film club, but the screen will be on the other wall and the seating will be luxurious. I want couples seating as well as singles and small tables for their snacks and drinks, and we'll have waitresses delivering that stuff and accepting payment with a card swipe. I've got a backer that will fund that transformation."

Brian was taking some notes in a ruled schoolbook and was nodding furiously.

"The Shisha lounge will also be upstairs and between the two areas we'll have Pete's bar area and a small kitchen, not open to the public though, just a dispensary for the waitress staff. We'll get Deepa to get a few quotes for putting a false floor over the old open space. Downstairs we'll have the e-games arena and the karaoke area as well as some lavvies and a washroom. What do you think?"

"I think it sounds expensive Chuds, how are you going to cover all this?"

"That's the beauty of this being a listed building Brian. There are grants available for almost all of the renovations, if it can be proven that it makes the building more safe even the false floor at circle seating level will be covered. The operators of the various modules will cover most of the building and decorating that is not approved and will recoup that from taxes and shared revenue such as drink sales etc."

"Chuds you really thought this through didn't you?"

"I try to surround myself with good people Brian that's why you're here."

"And there was me thinking it was my natural beauty and the earring."

"Let's walk up to the Regal and meet with Deepa, you'll like her, you might even remember her."

"How will I remember someone I've never met Chuds?"

"We'll see."

When they arrived at the site Deepa was standing outside holding three yellow hard hats. She offered one to each of the men, and put one on her own head. She looked every bit the professional lawyer, just with a yellow hat on.

"Chuds introduced Brian and Deepa pulled the "Nice to meet you. Again," line which you could tell confused the hell out of Brian. He mouthed at Chuds, "What the fuck?"

"Think hard Brian," and they followed the solicitor into the building.

The interior was a mess, but it was easy to see that it would not take too much to clear it back and start renovations. Chuds shared the ideas that he and Brian had discussed and Deepa made notes with a stylus on a tablet. They walked around the entire interior and Chuds explained where each module should be, even the stairs were still okay and they went up to the circle seating area.

"Deepa I want this whole space to be the film club. That's going to be my baby, we'll have a digital projection booth where the balcony is now and throw the movie onto a screen on that wall. I want full surround sound and seating so luxurious we'll have to throw the punters out. Across this void over the ground level seating I need a nice strong floor for the shisha lounge and catering areas, and fit restrooms in wherever you can."

Deepa was drawing diagrams and annotating them furiously and the trio made their way back downstairs. She looked up at Chuds and smiled.

"Chuds, this town needs this project. There used to be 4 or 5 cinemas in Gravesend but there hasn't even been one here for years, there's very little for people to do and I think you're going to provide some well needed entertainment for all ages. By the way, all of those grants that Anil told you about have been applied for, might take a few months to get approval, but he's very good at this stuff. If he wasn't sure it would be approved he wouldn't even apply."

"We can get financing to front the renovations Deepa, as long as we know there's Government money coming."

As they walked the floor level area Chuds explained where the e-Arena should be and what seating would be involved.

"We also need the highest speed internet connection available Deepa. Not mobile WiFi we need a wired connection with a back up. These guys play for big stakes and they play fast and hard. I never knew people would pay to watch other people play video games, but believe me they will."

"Oh I know Chuds, I stream games on Twitch all the time. Much better than what passes for TV."

"Well, we'll be streaming from here as well Deepa and these guys will also offer coaching and instruction. We need four of the biggest monitors you can get against that wall, the arena should be soundproofed and the sound system should be the best we can get. This has to be a totally immersive environment."

Pointing to the other half of the ground floor he outlined where the two party rooms should be, but capable of being opened into one big room. A Videoke system for each room. Then smaller rooms ranging in capacity from one person up to eight people.

"Wait I just got a message from Marti."

Chuds read the message and laughed loudly.

"She wants one room to be a shower with a waterproof videoke system, capable of holding two people. I told her the karaoke module was for people who wanted to sing, just not in the shower. She thinks we should offer that option, so that they can sing with accompaniment AND in the shower. Apparently she was upset that there might not be a truly adult component to her side of the business."

He looked at Deepa who was trying to suppress a laugh, "Cost it out Deepa, if we can do that it could be fun."

Deepa wrote on her tablet and said, "I can't wait to met this chick."

Chapter 30

That evening Brian and Chuds went to Pete's pub to chat with Mona about the Shisha Lounge. The pub was, as usual, fairly quiet with only a couple of small groups of people sitting at the tables. The two men sat at the bar and discussed the bar and catering options as well as trying to decide on a business name for the lounge.

"How about 'Hookahs'?" Mona suggested.

"Mo. We're trying to present an upscale image here. I want this lounge to exist on two levels. There will be those that come just for shisha, some nice chill music, healthy snacks and a relaxing time. Then, of course, there will be VIP areas for people to take one of the staff to and enjoy some private time, but I don't want that to be the focus. It should almost be our dirty little secret."

"That's my other name out the window then Chuds. You got any ideas?"

They all thought for a while, sipping on some drinks. Mona served one of the tables and Pete went upstairs to make a few sandwiches.

When he came back down Pete excitedly said, "Chuds, Brian, if we keep it in the Regal and Royal theme we could use something like 'The Maharaja's Lounge' couldn't we?"

"I like the thematic idea Pete, I really do. Let's toss a few ideas around like that. I'm also going to need an idea for a name for your module, even though the public won't be there, having the bar and food business as a separate company will make it a lot easier to allocate dividends to the other businesses. That way anyone that orders from, say the karaoke lounge, the karaoke business will get a dividend from that purchase. That will encourage all of the modules to push the food and drink."

"Oo, I like that," Pete looked positively gleeful.

Suddenly Mona banged her hand on the bar counter and yelled, "I got it!"

"I'm hardly surprised after all these years on the game Mona," Brian replied.

"Screw you Captain Slack Sparrow with your pirate earring. Chuds, I want to call it 'Sheikha's Shisha' what do you think."

Brian unconsciously fiddled with his new earring, but his expression said he liked the name.

"I love it Mona," Chuds gave her a thumbs up, "I'll text Anil now. Pete come on buddy we're waiting for you."

"Oh it's so hard Chuds."

Mona looked at him and said, "That's something you haven't said in a long while."

"You don't know everything about me you fat slag," and he kissed her on the cheek.

Looking at Chuds he reminded him that he had once managed a cinema in town.

"Yeah, the ABC Cinema, it was a 3 screen place when I ran it."

"What was it called before though?"

"The Majestic, it was called the Majestic! Okay I think I see where you're going."

"Kind of a tribute Chuds, can we call it 'The Majestic Kitchen Company', what do you think?"

Brian looked at him and said, "Well you are an old Queen Pete."

"Hush your mouth, I'm not THAT old."

Chuds sent another text to Anil who acknowledged receipt and promised to work on acquiring the company names tomorrow.

"That just leaves the e-arena and the karaoke business to name. My two e-athletes have said that we can choose their business name, apparently they "can't be arsed with it" or they're too busy shooting bad guys to deal with it, but anyway we have free reign on that."

Brian looked up sharply, 'Free Reign Gaming' Chuds. Keeps the Royal theme going and just for the record, I came up with it."

"Then that'll be it Bri. Now Karaoke, what can we use for that."

"Shouldn't you ask Marti?"

"Well technically it's Johnny Mowton's business, Marti will be a manager, maybe a partner, that's between her and Johnny."

Brian suggested a meeting between the four of them so Chuds called Johnny and Marti and suggested a meeting at the weekend. Marti was gigging on Friday so they agreed to meet at The Three Daws pub, just down the road from the Italian restaurant, during one of Johnny's set breaks on Saturday evening.

That meeting confirmed, Brian excused himself and said he was going to meet Brenda for a drink.

"You two back together then," asked Chuds.

"Working on it, I'm trying mate," and he left.

"I think I'll call it a night soon as well. Just top that Guinness off for me Mona, then I'll go back to the flat."

"I hear my Ro is helping you with some computer stuff Chuds, anything going on there? You know I called first dibs on you."

"Mona, honestly, she's young enough to be my daughter! Besides I don't think she likes me too much."

"She really don't like too many people Chuds, but if she hasn't stabbed you yet, she probably thinks you're alright."

"She sounds a keeper Mona, she really does. You going to use her at Sheikah's?"

"Of course I'll offer her something Chuds, but she's her own woman, it's up to her."

Chuds was really enjoying his new apartment and was even getting comfortable using the computer. IKEA delivered and assembled the office furniture and now he had a place to work and focus on the business.

He kept a journal and planner where he outlined and prioritized what needed to be done and despite Ro telling him that he could do all that in a spreadsheet, he liked his notebooks better. Checking through tasks he jotted down that Anil had secured the company names and Deepa told him that she had acquired the blueprints and plans for the original building, including the basement area where apparently an old Wurlitzer organ had been stored before.

Chuds asked her to plot out some office space and a secure area down there and tod her that he would catch up with her the following Monday.

Before that there was the meeting with Johnny and Marti to consider and he recorded the things he needed to get from that meeting. This included a company and business name and not least agreement between the two of them to work as a team.

On the evening of the meeting Chuds walked from his riverside flat along to the Three Daws, the pub rested by the Gravesend Pier and was reputed to be the oldest, still surviving pub in the town. Despite having grown up in the town and having run many businesses in the area he had never been in the pub before. It had obviously been renovated many times, and beautifully so, but the history was there.

With his love of the River and its history Chuds couldn't understand why he had never been in there before. Some historical notes were displayed on the walls as well as some beautiful images of the Thames. Apparently the history of the pub dated back to the 1400's and it had a special feel to it, it seemed to epitomize the old town and its relationship with the Thames and the sea.

He ordered himself a beer and grabbed a menu while he waited for Johnny and Marti to arrive. To his surprise they arrived together and joined him at his table. Chuds shook Johnny's hand and kissed Marti on the cheek before they all sat down together.

"You two know each other?" he asked generally.

Marti replied, "We didn't until tonight. I decided to go to the restaurant and check this guy out, he's a good performer."
Johnny looked at her then at Chuds, "And I recognized her straight away Chuds. You know who this is right?"

"Well actually Johnny we only just reconnected after almost 30 years," he winked at Marti, " I know who she was, but I kinda lost track of her career."

"Chuds, this is Marti Price, one of the most sought after session and backing vocalists in the business. She's been on more hit records than Elvis Presley and sung on almost every stage in the country."

Looking at his old friend Chuds seemed genuinely shocked, "Marti I had no idea, why didn't you tell me? Can we even afford you for this project?"

"Well Chuds, I didn't tell you because you never asked AND yes, I'm tired of touring, they want young girls up on the stage now and I'm looking for a steady gig. So yeah, you can probably afford me."

Chuds ordered a round of drinks and toasted to the new venture, all three glasses chinked and the final module was put in place for the Regal.

"Johnny, Marti we need a business and operating name for the karaoke module. We're trying to keep it in a Royal or Regal theme. Do either of you have any ideas?"

Both looked puzzled at first, then Johnny came up with 'Queen's Karaoke' as an idea because it would have a woman fronting the operation but Chuds was a little worried that people might link it to the band.

Marti wanted to use the word 'Sovereign' and eventually they came up with 'Sovereign's Song Palace' which both Chuds and Johnny agreed was both unusual enough to be attention catching yet kept in with the Royal theme.

"Does anybody need to sleep on this or can I send the name to Anil?"

Johnny and Marti looked at each other and both smiled at the same time.

"Go for it Chuds, as long as it's available get your solictor to register it. Now if you'll excuse us, Marti is going to do my second set with me at Giovanni's."

"That's awesome, I'm so happy that you two get along, I have a really good feeling about this venture. So, how are things at the restaurant?"
"Well they miss you for sure Chuds. I don't think they ever had a dishwasher as efficient as you were. The place is busy though, but that guy Basha is bringing the tone down and creating some problems for Steve."

"Why, what's happening?"

'He's bringing girls in the place that look about 14 Chuds, if that. They sit at the table with him and he tells Steve that they're his niece or cousin or some distant relation, but often other men come and sit with them for a while, then the guy will leave with the young girl. It's only happened a couple of times at the weekends when I'm there but one of the waitresses said it happens quite a bit on weekdays. They're kids Chuds and I think he's renting them out, makes me sick. I'm tempted to quit that gig, I don't want to be anywhere near things like that."

"Can't say I blame you Johnny, but hang in there I think his time might be about up."

Marti gave Chuds the side eye and said, "You're not going to do anything that we might all regret are you?"

"Me Marti? I have no idea what you mean, I'm a changed man."

"You better be Mister, I'm looking forward to this gig."

"Hey Johnny, did you know that Chuds used to be a bass player?"

Johnny looked surprised but before he could say anything Chuds interrupted, "I wouldn't say I was a bass player exactly, although I did know which way round to hold it."

"You weren't bad Chuds, you weren't good either, but definitely not bad. We used to be in a band together for a while"

Johhny looked intrigued, "Maybe you should think about getting the band back together Marti."

"Johnny, I haven't touched a bass guitar in so long I doubt I'd know which end to blow into. Plus at least two of the old crew are dead now. Best to leave those days in my past and let the real musicians do their thing now."

Chapter 31

Marti and Johnny walked back up to the restaurant and Chuds stayed behind in the pub. As they walked up the High Street Johnny asked, "What was all that about Chuds being a changed man?"

"Let's just say that he has a chequered past. He used to be what you might call a 'Jack the Lad' back in the day. He had interests in a lot of businesses, some of them legit and many of them not. It was always hard to tell exactly how he was involved, but he usually was. Some used to call him 'The King of Gravesend' but I wouldn't do that if I was you. He hated it then and probably still does."

"He sounds like a really interesting character Marti, I'm glad we're working with him."

"Let's hope you still feel that way in a couple of years time."

Sitting in the pub, Chuds sent texts to Anil regarding the business names and to Deepa asking for another site visit on Monday. Then he sent a text to Mona asking if she knew the whereabouts of their old friend Marvin, from the local CID.

Mona called him back a few minutes later and suggested that he come to Pete's pub and she would try and find out where he was. She mentioned that Ro was there and wanted a word with him as well.

He finished his beer and walked the quarter mile or so to Pete's place. For a Saturday night the place had a fair crowd in and both Pete and Mona were working behind the bar. Ro was sitting on a stool at the far end of the bar and Chuds waked over to join her.

As he sat down next to her she smiled at him, the first time he had ever really seen her smile, and she asked him why he was looking for Starvin' Marvin.

"Oh yeah we did call him that didn't we? Skinniest fucker I ever knew, looked like a famine victim. I'd really just like to catch up, he was always fair to us. Knew when to look the other way"

"Well, I'm not sure I believe that reason Chuds, but Mum got a number for you. He's retired from the Police now and runs a security and private investigator company in the Bexley area," she slid a piece of paper across to Chuds, "Here's his number anyway."

"Thanks Ro," and looking at Mona he showed her the piece of paper and mouthed, "Thanks Mo."

She gave him a big smile while pulling pints for a customer at the bar.

"How come you're in the pub Ro, Saturday night I thought you'd be working the other job."

"It's getting tough now Chuds, half the time I go to a hotel or a bar some big fucker tries to scare off the punters, I'm sure it's Basha's people. Never any real trouble they just come right up and stand next to me while I'm offering a deal, kind of intimidate the punters. There's only a few of us freelancers left now, Basha's running almost all the girls. And when I say girls, I mean it Chuds, fucking young teenagers, look like they should still be in school."

"I heard a little something about that. Sorry you're having problems Ro, anything you think I can do."

"I wish there was Chuds but I have no idea what. Anyway I wanted to ask you something."

"Sure Ro, fire away."

"It seems like your new business venture is well under way," Chuds nodded and smiled, "As you know I'm pretty handy with a computer and I did some courses on coding and web design. I wanted to know if you'd be interested in hiring me as a media manager, I can build and host a website for you and manage your social media accounts."

"Oh thank God!" Chuds looked genuinely relieved, "As you know Ro, I am fucking useless at anything like that. The two guys that are running the e-arena asked me who was going to run the social media accounts and I honestly didn't have a clue what they meant."

"Chuds, there's almost no such thing as a local paper any more and the only viable place to advertise and promote your product is online. I'm not saying it's a good thing or a bad thing, but it IS a thing and you're going to need to target your posts to the people that you want to attract. You need Twitter, Instagram and Facebook accounts for the business and a dynamic website that will pull people in."

"Yeah, what you said Ro, you're hired."

"We haven't talked money yet Chuds, you do know I'm a business woman, right?" she winked at him, "How much you offering"

"How much do you want?"

She leaned in and whispered in his ear, Chuds pretended to look shocked and shook his head, then stuck his hand out and repeated, "You're hired!"

Before their hands separated Mona leaned across the bar and put two fresh drinks in front of both of them. Looking at Chuds Mona said, "You won't regret this Chuds, she's an online wizard."

They raised their glasses at Mona and Pete and toasted Ro's new appointment.

Ro asked him to get her a set of keys for his apartment.
"Um why?"

"I'm going to need to work out of your office Chuds and use your laptop."

"Couldn't you just take the laptop with you and work from home or from the cafe?"

"Where would be the fun in that Chuds, besides I kind of like hanging out with you."

Mona had overheard the conversation and tipped Chuds an exaggerated wink, Chuds looked back and mouthed "Fuck you."

Mona threw her head back and said, "You wish, but looks like you might be keeping it in the family."

Chuds blushed a little and quickly sipped some more of his drink. Ro looked very pleased with herself and said, "You can drop those keys in the cafe any time Chuds."

"I suppose I can Ro, fuck me this seems to be getting out of hand. What will I need to do, tie something to the door handle if I have some female company?"

"As if."

Chapter 32

On Sunday morning Chuds dialled the number Mona had gotten for Starvin' Marvin, it was an office number and unsurprisingly went through to a voice mail system. It sounded very professional and Chuds left a nice message asking to speak to Marvin at his earliest convenience.

He walked to the hardware department at the huge supermarket and had a set of keys made for Ro which he took to her at the coffee shop and even as he handed them over to her, he wondered if this was a mistake. She made him a cappuccino and toast which he enjoyed while sitting by the window in his usual spot.

As it was Sunday the street was quiet and he pulled out his notebook and started looking through the to-do lists. It was amazing how quickly all of this was coming together. Depending on the outcome of the upcoming site visit with Deepa and how long the renovations would take he could imaging the venue opening in about one month.

He knew that she already had a crew inside clearing out the rubble and debris and had booked surveys from a sprinkler company and an insurance assessor to keep the policies in line with the changing value of the property. She really seemed to be on top of the job and he was grateful to Anil for letting her work this project.

Brian still had no idea where Deepa claimed to know him from, and Chuds thought that was delicious. He was, however, so impressed with the way Brian had started recovering from his depression. It seemed that a focussed project was what he really needed, and he was doing such a great job.

Still sipping his coffee, his phone rang and although he didn't recognize the number he answered it anyway.

"Chuds Douglas?"

"Speaking."

"Chuds you old villain, Marvin here. How have you been?"

Chuds stared to fill him in on his adventures and told him that the next project in his life was shaping up well, without revealing too many details. Marvin revealed that he had left the force, taken an early retirement and now ran his own small security company.

"I do a bit of PI Work on the side too Chuds, but none of that divorce shit, just tracking people down and getting intel for companies."

"Marvin, I may need your security services once my new project gets ready to open, but also I was wondering if you could do a little digging on a local enterprise for me?"

"Let me guess Chuds, The Basha family."

"What are you? Telepathetic now? How would you know that?"

"Chuds, part of being successful in my business is knowing what goes on. I heard about your barney with Basha Junior, and how's your mate Ronnie doing?"

"Ronnie is recovering okay Marv, not sure what his future is with me, but we're still talking. I got a tip that Basha is still gunning for me, and I'm trying to find a way to neutralize that."

"Chuds, he seems pretty bulletproof. The local bill know what he's up to but seem to think it's okay to let him carry on."

"I heard some disturbing stories about him using young girls as escorts Marvin, even if I didn't have beef with him I'd be trying to stop that."

"I have some contacts at the NCA Chuds, I can do some digging, but I can't do it for free."

"I wouldn't expect you to Marvin, a friend tells me he's getting more and more brazen and even fixing up 'dates' in a restaurant, in full view of everyone. Marv, I don't really have any transport at the moment, any chance you can come down to Gravesend and we'll have a meet up?"

"Sure Chuds, checking my calendar now, how would Wednesday morning around 10:30 work for you?"

"Sounds good I'll text you my address, I have a small office in my flat, we can meet there."

As he finished his coffee, Ro brought him another and sat opposite him.

"Chuds you know I told you I was getting some aggro from some of Basha's crew when I'm trying to work a hotel or pub?"

"Yeah, anything happen to you?"

"Aw, you care. Not me Chuds a friend, she was moving on a potential customer and as they went to leave the pub a thug started pushing her around. He didn't bruise her up or anything but he scared her shitless and the punter ran off like a frightened rabbit. He knocked her to the ground, didn't say a word, just turned her over a little and walked away."

"Need an escort next time you go out Ro? I'll come with you if you like, or get you a minder from Marvin."

"I'd rather it was you Chuds, would you? I was thinking of trying my luck again tonight at that new hotel. It was good for me last time."

"Of course Ro, what time?"

"I'll aim to get there around 10:00, they've had a few drinks by then and more likely to be looking for some company."

"I'll be there ahead of you Ro, sitting at the bar with a tonic water."

That night at 9:30 pm found Chuds sitting at the hotel bar, he had scoped out the area and positioned the rest rooms, the 2 exit doors, one into the hotel lobby and one to the exterior grounds and the couple of small alcoves, one of which already three people sitting at it. At the opposite end of the bar sat a large man, not one that Chuds had seen before but he did seem a little out of place.

In front of Chuds was a glass of tonic water with ice and lemon and a hotel key card, he had booked a small room so that he looked more natural sitting at the bar alone. Just another traveller.

At around 9:45 Ro walked in the door, Chuds smiled, she looked nice, well dressed, a couple of tattoos visible and there was that ear thing, however she looked good, and confident. Her eye caught Chuds and she didn't acknowledge him outwardly, just a hint of a smile like she might give any potential customer.

Chuds noticed the man at the bar stare at her and adjust his position on his bar stool. Ro sat at the bar and looked around the room, she walked over to Chuds and started talking to him as if he was a mark.

"The guy at the end of the bar is one of Basha's men Chuds, pretend I'm hitting on you then reject me, I can take it," and she giggled.

He spoke a few sentences then shook his head emphatically, Ro walked back to her seat. She ordered a glass of wine and waited. Occasionally looking around the room, she sipped slowly, Chuds noticed that every time she took a sip, some wine went back into the glass. This girl was not going to get drunk.

After twenty minutes or so a middle aged business man came into the bar from the hotel lobby and sat close to Ro. She smiled at him and raised her glass, and he smiled in return. Within five minutes he had moved down and was sitting next to her, he had bought her another wine, which so far sat untouched, and they appeared to be enjoying their conversation.

The business man called the bartender and signed his bill to his room account and smiling at Ro started to get up.

Which way they were going would dictate what happened next. Would they walk to the river for some fresh air or would they go through the hotel lobby and straight to a room? Basha's man at the end of the bar shuffled in his seat, obviously waiting for the same information and when he saw them walk towards the exterior he stood up and started to follow them. He would have to walk right past Chuds.

Chuds put his phone in his pocket and just as Basha's man was behind him he dropped the key card to the floor. He bent down to pick it up, stumbled into the man's path and then stood quickly, knocking him backwards. The man tried to keep his balance but Chuds grabbed his jacket and while it looked like he was trying to help, he slipped his left foot behind the man's ankle and pushed with his palm.

He fell backwards and Chuds slipped to one knee, apologizing loudly to the man but holding him down on the carpet. He looked over his shoulder and Ro and her client were already outside.

He apologized again to the man who was trying to get up, Chuds stood and held out his hand to help, which the man brushed aside. He looked for Ro and the business man then started to walk outside to see where they were, Chuds pulled a small bunch of keys from his pocket and, rattling them loudly shouted, "Hey, you dropped these!"

The man looked around at Chuds and then back to the door starting to walk outside, Chuds followed him out yelling, "You dropped your keys."

Once outside Chuds ran at the man full speed and shoulder charged him in the back. He went down hard and Chuds brought his foot down with force onto the back of his neck. The man's arms were out to his side and Chuds turned and stamped as forcefully as he could onto one of the man's wrists, then knelt heavily on the same arm. He pushed the man's head into the ground and whispered, "Stay down, you're done for the night."

"Fuck you," but his face was pressed so hard onto the car park pavement that it was hard to understand.

Grabbing a handful of hair Chuds pulled the man's head of the ground then smashed it back onto the asphalt. He heard and felt the man's nose break as he grunted a muffled scream. Reaching into his jacket pocket Chuds pulled out a heavy duty zip tie, roughly pulled the man's arms behind his back and cuffed his wrists together. One was already swelling where he had stamped on it.

Then he rolled him over onto his back. The man was conscious but barely, probably only the pain stopping him from passing out. Looking around there was nobody else in the car park, but there were a couple of cctv cameras.

That couldn't be helped, Chuds had deliberately kept his back to them as much as possible, and knowing who the man on the ground worked for he doubted the police would be too interested in identifying him.

Chapter 33

Surprisingly the next few days passed without any signs of repercussions from Basha. When Chuds visited Ro at the coffee shop she greeted him with, "My hero," to which he took a small bow and accepted a complimentary cappuccino. It appeared that only one of her friends had gone out working in the last couple of days and had experienced no intimidation.

Ro made arrangements to visit with Chuds that night to discuss a social media strategy and informed him that he already had an Instagram account called @RegalModularEntertainment.

"If I knew what that was I'd be impressed Ro, we can talk it all through this evening if you like."

"Okay Chuds, and I mean this, thanks for looking out for me the other night."

"Any time Ro, you take care, I can get you and the girls minders if you like."

"Hopefully we won't need it Chuds, but I appreciate it. Now I know why my Mum speaks so highly of you."

The site visit with Deepa was also very productive, the various entertainment modules were clearly marked out and the new floor from the circle seating area was already under construction.

Chuds went down into the basement area and was surprised how much room was down there. He didn't remember it being this big from before. Disappointingly the old Wurlitzer was gone, but there was an abundance of space for storage and a small suite of offices. He agreed to plan something out but told Deepa to make sure that the sprinkler system was extended into the whole basement area immediately.

That evening, as arranged, Ro arrived at the apartment, and rang the building's front doorbell then getting Chuds to let her in.

"Why did I even give you a set of keys if you're going to ring the doorbell?"

"We haven't firmed up that 'tie on the door handle' protocol yet, I didn't want to intrude."

"I appreciate that, so let's get to work shall we?"

She took out her phone, opened Instagram and showed Chuds his first ever post. Which even though he hadn't made it, somehow made him feel proud of his project. It was an impressive promo piece outlining the four main entertainment modules that would be in the new property.

"That's really nice Ro, but I'm not sure that I want this much info out there just yet."

"That's the beauty of social media Chuds, we tell them just as much as we want them to know. This account is private right now, people have to ask to follow you, we will change all that once we're ready to start a real push."

"Nice, so what else do we need to do?"

Ro explained that she should register some domain names for the four modules and the master company and select a provider to host the site.

"I think to start with Chuds we will need just one site and have all the domain names point to it. No matter what people search for and whichever link they click it will take them to the main site, then they can dive deeper and visit the sub-site that they want. That way all the master promo will be on the home pages, and won't clutter up the individual businesses."

"I'm pretty sure I get what you mean Ro. Can you design all this and make all the hosting arrangements?"

"Sure can Chuds, now let's chat about Twitter and Facebook."

They talked for over two hours about the marketing strategy, and it was without doubt the longest conversation he had ever held with the girl. She was knowledgable and explained things very clearly, she was also very comfortable to be with.

Halfway through the meeting she asked if he had wine. Walking to the fridge and opening the door he asked, "Red or White?"

She looked up from the laptop and replied, "Yes please."

"Red it is then," pulling the bottle from the rack he said, "I keep my Red wine cool, is that wrong?"

"Chuds, I'm a working girl not a sommelier, just pour me a glass, and don't cheap out on the serving."

She went over several options regarding presenting the business online, defining the different age demographics for the various options and laying out a provisional timetable for starting the campaigns.

"You don't want to push this too early Chuds, or people will be bored with it before you open the doors, but we can't leave it too late either. We will really need to work on the timing, and also consult with your gamer boys on what image they want to present, same with my Mum and your karaoke guy."

"I think meetings with each group individually Ro, better to get their focus without the other businesses influencing them."

"Agreed, but they are going to have to conform to a common theme Chuds, you want people to know it's all under one brand."

"I'm so glad I hired you Ro."

"And I thank you for giving me the opportunity."

They chinked their glasses together and drained them, before Chuds went off to get the bottle and refill.

"Chuds, I can get another girl to open the coffee shop tomorrow, I would really love to start on this properly in the morning, any chance I can work here tomorrow?"

"I've got a meeting with a security company at 10 Ro."

"It's okay, I'll be quiet."

"Well I suppose I could meet with him in the living room. Sure what time do you want to come tomorrow?"

"I was wondering if I could stay over Chuds, don't want to risk going home alone at night after that business at the hotel."

"Wow, you sprung that on me Ro, I suppose you could crash on the couch if you really want to."

"Cheers Chuds, now let's wrap this up so I can make a clean start in the morning."

They finished their meeting, drank a little more wine and Chuds got her a towel, a blanket and a pillow from the closet which he placed on the couch.

"Please tell me you don't snore Ro."

"I've never heard myself snore, but I ain't promising."

Chapter 34

When Chuds got up the next morning and went through to the living room, Ro was already up and making a pot of coffee. She was wearing just a t-shirt and looked for all the world like she belonged in the apartment. They both grunted a good morning greeting and she carried 2 mugs over to the table. They drank in silence, looking out over the river.

"Not really a morning person Ro?"

"Neither am I Chuds."

"I meant... oh never mind. Thanks for the coffee."

She carried the pot over and refreshed their mugs, they drank more coffee before she eventually said that she should shower and get dressed. Grabbing the towel and her backpack she walked off to the bathroom and Chuds seriously wondered what was happening here.

When she came out, showered and dressed in clean clothes she simply said, "I'll crack on in the office then."

Chuds drained his mug, washed both of them and showered himself.

His phone beeped for a notification and it was Marvin saying he was about 15 minutes out, Chuds did a miniscule amount of tidying and waited for his old friend. At almost exactly 10:00 the entrance buzzer sounded and Chuds let Marvin in. He opened the apartment door and saw a man who weighed at least 280 lbs struggle up the steps. Doing a double take to make sure this was Marvin he quipped, "I guess you're not Starvin' any more eh?"

"Nice of you to be so tactful Chuds, yeah the years have been good to me, I put on a little weight."

"A little?"

"Come on in Marvin, it's good to see you again, all of you."

Once she heard Marvin come in Ro left the office and introduced herself, offering coffee, tea or water.

"Ro is my Marketing Manager, Marvin, and shouldn't be doing coffees, she's proven herself to be invaluable."

"Oh I don't mind Chuds, Marvin?"

"I'd love a coffee please."

She went over to the kitchen and Marvin and Chuds started catching up. Marvin explained his new business and showed a list of his current and past clients for security services and offered a small brochure outlining the PI services offered.

In turn, Chuds explained his new business and said he would be interested in having 24 hour security at the new venue once it opened.

"Remember Brian?"

"Of course, how is he nowadays?"

"He's doing okay, he'll be running the day to day Marvin, I'll arrange a meeting nearer the opening date."

"Great Chuds, I can offer a full CCTV package as well, monitored off site for extra security."

"Talking of CCTV, are you doing security at the River View hotel?"

"We are."

"Any chance you could make a bit of footage from the car park 2 nights ago vanish."

"Funny thing Chuds, those cameras weren't working that night," and he winked, then looking at Ro he said, "knew I recognized you Miss."

Ro made a half smile half scowl expression and went back to the office.

"Chuds I've been doing a bit of digging, I've got some information but we need to sign a legal contract with you hiring my company. We have to establish a legal partnership and all that entails."

"Not a problem Marvin, you have one drawn up?"

"I do, indeed."

Contracts signed and a handshake cementing the deal, Marvin leaned in and started to tell Chuds what he had found out.

Basha was bringing in young girls as nieces or cousins of family members for holidays. They would stay for 90 days then leave, ostensibly to return to Albania, but with a little digging it seems they often headed for the Middle East, or South East Asia on different visas.

"Marvin, this is the very definition of trafficking. How is he getting away with this?"

"That is the million dollar question Chuds. I suspect palms are being greased or some blackmailing is going on."

"Marvin, you know that I'm no angel, but this 'Basha'll fix it' business is really not on."

"I agree. Chuds you may have poked a hornet's nest here. For some reason he thinks you pose a threat to his livelihood. I don't think he gives a crap about what you did to his son, who as we speak is probably recruiting more young girls, but he is worried that you are impacting his business here."

"Marvin, for now, keep digging for dirt. Do you remember my solicitor, Anil?"

"Sure do, I hear he's come up in the world."

"He's doing okay for sure. Send him a retaining invoice and he'll sort out your fees. Now, how about lunch? Want to go visit Poncy Pete and have some pub grub? I'll text Brian to join us, he'd love to see you I'm sure."

"Damn that sounds good, haven't seen that old queen or Brian for many years."

Chuds called out to Ro and they all walked down the riverfront to Pete's pub. When they entered the door Pete let out one of his trademark squeals and rushed over to hug Chuds. Fat Mona turned to look at who had come in and gasped, "Marvin? Starvin' Marvin?"

"Not so hungry these days Mona, damn it 's good to see you again," and he did what he could to lean across the bar and kiss her cheek.

"I see you already met my daughter," and she pointed at Ro.

"Your daughter? I had no idea Mona, damn she's a good looking girl, a real chip off the old block."

"Steady Marv, I think she's got a little significant other action brewing, stand down."

"I'm happily married Mona, besides, look at me."

"Hang on, I'll get a wide angle lens."

They all sat around a table and Pete went off to make sandwiches, and over more drinks they reminisced about the old days. After about 20 minutes Marvin leaned over to Chuds and whispered, "Your 6 o'clock Chuds, one of Basha's guys?"

Waiting a few minutes Chuds glanced around the bar discretely before nodding. A few minutes later Brian arrived and there was more hugging and hand shaking. Chuds called over to Pete and asked if they could borrow Mona for a business chat, and they all sat around the pub table with multiple conversations covering old experiences.

Finally Chuds managed to bring the conversation round to the new business and explained what had been discussed with Ro regarding marketing and branding.

"I need a theme Mona, I want to keep colour schemes within a range of blues through purples, so what are your thoughts?"

"I think we should loosely model the interiors on neo-middle eastern décor Chuds. Modern themes but with a nod to the Shisha heritage. The VIP rooms should be very luxurious, with couches like they have in a Middle East Majilis, and lots of curtains. Also a really nice sound system playing Said Mrad, Saad Chishty, cool electronica with nice relaxing beats."

"Sounds great Mona, you've put a lot of thought into it haven't you, can you jot that all down so we can get it costed and run it all past Deepa?"

"What did you think Chuds? That it would just be me doing the dance of the seven veils?"

Brian looked up sharply and said, "You'd need a lot more than seven veils Mona."

"Fuck you Long Dong Silver, I'm gonna make this place classy, so classy you wouldn't understand."

"I got class Mona, it's all low, I'll grant you that, but it's class."

They raised their glasses and chinked them together. Marvin looked over at Chuds and nodded towards Basha's man who was just leaving.

"I've gotta go anyway Chuds, I'll call you tomorrow."

"Great to see you Marvin," and they all waved as he left the pub.

Mona went back behind the bar, Brian left to visit the new building and Ro and Chuds decided to go back and discuss the online marketing. As they were leaving Mona called out, "Behave yourselves you two. Or not," and she winked at Ro who just said "Mum!"

Chapter 35

They worked on the marketing strategies until about 9:00 pm, and went through another bottle of wine. Chuds was finding it incredibly interesting and cold see why this was such an important part of the business.

As they wrapped up, he looked over at Ro and started to speak, but before he could say anything she interrupted, "It's alright Chuds, I gotta go anyway, I need some clean knickers."

"At least let me order you a taxi Ro,"

"That'd be nice, thanks."

After she left, Chuds took his shower and went straight to bed, he drifted easily into a deep sleep. A sleep that he was woken from in the early hours of the morning by sirens screaming past his apartment. He glanced at the clock, it was a little after 3:00 am, once the noise subsided he tried to get back to sleep, but it took a long while.

He woke at his usual time of 6:30 and did not feel especially rested. He needed coffee and he needed it now, he grabbed his phone and walked out to the kitchen to brew a pot. The blinking light on his phone indicated a text and he opened the app.

The message was from Marvin asking him to call as soon as possible, however he waited until the coffee was brewed and had poured himself a mug, then made the call.

"Chuds?"

"Marvin, what's up?"

"You okay Chuds?"

"Not bad for an old guy that only just opened his eyes, what's the matter Marv?"

"Chuds, there was a fire last night at Pete's pub, it burned to the ground."

"Fuck! Marvin, how's Pete, he okay?

"He's in the hospital Chuds, smoke inhalation and a couple of burns, but he's just in for observation, but Chuds..."

"What?"

"Mona couldn't get out Chuds, she apparently had a sleep disorder and Pete couldn't wake her, she's gone buddy, I'm so sorry."

"Gone? Mona? What the fuck Marvin? Do they know what caused the fire?"

"The investigators are still there Chuds, look you need to take care of her girl. The cops are notifying her but you should be there for her."

"I'll get her here now Marvin. Keep me informed about the investigation."

"Will do Chuds, you have Ro's address?

"Yeah it's on her contract, Marvin thanks for being the one to tell me."

He called Brian and told him to visit Pete in the hospital and to get back in touch with Marvin and have a security man on the ward just in case. He told Brian to make sure that Pete was okay and safe and to get him anything he needed, then he ordered a taxi to take him to Ro's place.

When he arrived at Ro's place a policeman was standing at the door, Chuds identified himself and explained that Ro worked for him, he let him through and a policewoman was sitting on the couch next to her, an arm around her shoulder and Ro was sobbing, deeply sobbing.

She looked up, saw Chuds and ran to him, throwing her arms around his neck and crying into his shoulder.

"Mum's gone Chuds, why my Mum? Why Chuds?"

Chuds pulled her in really tight and said, "I don't know Ro, but I promise I'll find out what happened."

She kept sobbing until the tears had dried up, yet she kept holding him tight, "Promise me you'll find out Chuds, make me that promise."

"Oh I will, grab some clothes Ro, you're coming home with me, and you can even have the bed this time, I'll take the couch."

"You're a fucking Prince, Chuds Douglas," but she kept the hug going for a long time.

The taxi had been waiting outside and after Ro had grabbed a small case of clothes and make up they took the cab back to Chuds apartment. They poured some wine and sat on the small balcony, feeling the river, listening to the waters lap over the shore, watching some boats and a few swans.

"You need anything, and I mean anything, you just tell me, okay Ro. I loved your Mum and I love you too and you can stay here as long as you like."

"I really appreciate it Chuds, I really do," and she stared into the river.

Brian called to report on Pete, "He's a fucking mess Chuds. Blames himself for not getting Mona out, he's feeling guilty about surviving when she didn't and he's crying non-stop."

"I'll call him later Brian, thanks buddy, you get Marvin to put a man on the ward?"

"All sorted Boss."

Several people called to offer their condolences, Anil offered to take care of all the arrangements and legal stuff and Ronnie called to see if there was anything he could do.

"You can listen Ronnie. If you hear anything, and I mean anything, that suggests that this wasn't an electrical fault or an accident you call me."

"On my life Chuds, if I hear anything you'll be the first to know."

"I'd better be Ronnie."

He poured Ro another wine and made some sandwiches. She drank the wine but didn't eat anything.

They watched the sun set and the lights of Tilbury come on. More boats made their way down the river and without even knowing how it had happened, Chuds realized that he was holding her hand. He didn't let go.

At around 10 she asked to go to bed, and Chuds walked her through to the bedroom, made sure that she had everything that she needed and turned to leave.

"Where the fuck do you think you're going Chuds Douglas?"

"To the couch Ro, the room's yours."

"Get back in here. You said that anything I needed I could have, well I need holding tonight Chuds, and you're on call. Get your ass in that bed."

Chuds stripped down to his underwear and climbed into the bed. Ro laid her head on his shoulder and he pulled her in tight. He felt her sob a few times, then heard her breathing settle and she fell asleep in his arms.

The next morning, when he woke, she was gone. Panicking slightly he got up, pulled on a t-shirt and some sweatpants and walked out into the living room. Ro was already on the balcony sipping from a mug of freshly brewed coffee.

"Chuds, get a coffee and come sit with me, I need to talk to you."

He did as she asked and sat beside her on the balcony, looking out over the river almost exactly as they had the previous evening.

"Thanks for staying with me last night, it meant a lot Chuds. I've got a lot to say here, so let me finish without interruption, okay?"

He nodded agreement and she started talking to him, without diverting her gaze from the river.

"Me and my Mum, we weren't that close Chuds, not like some mother and daughter acts, but I loved her and I respected her. She taught me a lot about life and business, especially our business. One of the things she was very adamant about was that we should always take care of our customers, they put the food on our table and the money in our piggy banks she would say."

"If you was serviced by my Mum, or me for that matter, you felt like you were a friend, not a punter. She made sure they were happy and cared for and that they would come back again and again. She had more regular punters than anyone I ever knew."

"She was really gung-ho about your new project Chuds, she talked about it all the time. She had a notebook of colour schemes, themed objects, a playlist of background music and a list of wholesale suppliers of Shisha. She really wanted this to work Chuds, she had girls lined up, training in Hookah use planned, an extra services menu for the girls to follow and everything. I want to take it over, for her Chuds, for her."

He waited to see if she had finished and should reply, she had not.

"I heard a lot about you Mr. Douglas, from an early age she would talk so highly of you, how you looked after the girls, made them feel safe, let them keep most of the proceeds. If one of her girls ever said that you was a Prince, she would correct them and tell'em you're a King amongst men, not a lowly Prince. Chuds I just wanna ask a couple of things from you. Let me take over Sheikha's Shisha, I'll do the marketing as well. The other thing is I want you to really find out what happened to my Mum and make it right. Can you do that?"

"I can, and I will Ro, I promise. You know how much I loved your Mum, we were best friends for a long time. I do need to ask you to do one thing for me though, whatever I find out, you need to let me deal with it. I don't need you charging around making the waters muddy and getting into trouble, promise you'll let me deal with whatever we find out."

"I promise Chuds, I'm a lover not a fighter. That hard girl act at the cafe is just that, an act."

He took her hand and gave it a squeeze, for the first time that morning she looked at him and smiled.

When his phone rang, it was Marvin. He asked after Ro and told Chuds that the investigation was still ongoing but he would let him have any information that he got the very moment that he got it. Chuds asked him if he could supply a security guard, in case things got a little hairy and to keep an eye on Ro.

"Funny you should say that Chuds, I got just the guy, says he knows you."

"That may not be such a good thing Marv."

"Oh I think this one will be. He told me to ask if you remembered a Greg Wallace."

"Wild Man Wallace? French Foreign Legion Greg Wallace?"

"That'd be him, he's called Francois Trouver now, got French Nationality when he left the service, said you worked together in Sudan."

"You know I can't comment on that Marvin, but I DO know a Wild Man Wallace. Tall, blond hair, Midlands accent?"

"That's him, I want to make him your head of security."

"He's hired, find him a room to stay down here and send him as soon as you can Marvin."

"Consider it done Chuds. I'm finding out some interesting information about your friend Basha, but I want to get it all sorted before I tell you too much, look tell Ro I'm thinking about her and that I'll help you get to the bottom of this."

He told Ro that he had a few calls to make, offered her breakfast, which she declined, and went back to the office.

Chapter 36

Making a list in his planner of those that he needed to call, he prioritized them and started dialling. He called Ronnie, he needed to keep a hand on his shoulder and make sure that he was listening for information, he called Pete at the hospital who still sounded rough but said he was feeling a little better and told Chuds to get Anil to come see him.

So he called Anil who promised to go that morning.

"I'm going to stay here and keep an eye on Ro, let me know what comes up. Tell Deepa I trust her and she should make any judgement calls regarding the building, I'll back her up all the way."

With the calls finished he went back to the kitchen, scrambled some eggs and made a fresh pot of coffee. He carried them through to Ro who hadn't moved and he put a plate of food and a mug of coffee in front of her.

"Eat that Ro, you're not doing yourself any favours by starving your self. I'll sit here until you're ready to do something different."

"I'll eat it Chuds, just for you, then I want to get on with some work. I want to start on the planning for the Shisha Lounge."

"Whenever you're ready. I've got a minder coming to help us with security, he'll end up running the security at the site but for now he'll help us out and make sure that we stay out of trouble."

She nodded that she understood and started to slowly eat her eggs.

After finishing her breakfast she looked at Chuds, "My Mum had a few business interests, that coffee shop is one of them and I think she had a few others around as well. I think Pete looked after everything for her, he's good with money and she trusted him."

Chuds told her that Pete had asked to see Anil presumably about her Mum's affairs, so she agreed to wait.

"Chuds, how long can I stay here with you?"

"As long as you like Ro, think of this as your home."

"I'm going to take a shower in my bathroom then Chuds. Get dressed you slob, I want to go see the new building and the layout for my new Shisha Lounge."

While she showered he called Deepa and told her that they would be visiting the site, she agreed to join them there. When she finished he stood to go to the bathroom and watched as Ro made the walk from the shower to the bedroom wearing only a small pair of panties.

"I guess she feels at home," Chuds muttered as he went to shower and dress.

They walked up the incline of the High Street and as they passed the coffee shop Ro waved at a young girl behind the counter. Three customers were sipping coffees and eating pastries and as they continued past, the shop Ro slipped her arm into Chuds and the turned onto New Road and headed towards the building.

They saw Deepa standing outside holding yellow hard hats and she greeted them, kissing Ro on the cheek and offering her condolences before shaking Chuds' hand. Chuds was surprised to see that so much clearance had already taken place and he told Deepa that Ro was now in charge of the Shisha Lounge and that she should follow her instruction on the layout and décor.

Because the new floor was still in the planning and preliminary stages she suggested that they simulate the layout on the ground floor, where the Karaoke Suite would eventually be. They walked the area, Ro was plotting a diagram in her notebook, Deepa was helping her with building and planning requirements and the two ladies seemed to be getting on really well. Chuds stepped back, looked up at the roof and sighed. This was one of his dreams, to renovate this place, and at last it was going to happen.

A little later Anil joined them, he had just got back from the hospital, and they looked over the sketches together. Finally Anil said, "Ro I just got back from visiting Pete, he gave me the number of a solicitor in Dartford that has your Mum's will and accounts details. He said it's all pretty sketchy, more a series of notes but it's quite clear that you are her only heir, and whatever was hers, is going to be yours after any taxes and legal fees."

"I'd rather have her back," Ro said, "but I'll take whatever she offered for me gratefully."

"I understand how you feel Ro, give me the rest of the day to sort through the info and we can meet tomorrow afternoon if you'd like to discuss it all."

They agreed on a time to meet the next day and Ro asked Chuds if they could go back to the flat, she needed some quiet time and wanted to remember her Mum.

They retraced their steps and walked back down New road and into the High Street, but as they passed the cafe Chuds saw the big bodyguard that had been with Bash Basha sitting in the cafe.

Chuds turned to Ro and told her, "I need you to go stand in that shop doorway opposite. Stay there until I come over to you and no matter what you see or what you think you see, just stay there, okay?"

"Everything okay Chuds?" she looked frightened, he nodded and guided her across the street.

Walking into the cafe Chuds stormed to the table and asked the man what he wanted, but he made it look like he was threatening him. The big guy stood quickly and pointed his finger at Chuds' chest in a threatening manner.

"A job really, Mr Douglas, I didn't sign up for a turf war and even if I had I wouldn't pick the side I find myself on."

They continued to point and look threatening so that anyone observing would think they were arguing.

"I might have something, but I've already got a security man starting soon, but if you keep your ear to the ground and let me know if you hear anything about the fire at the pub, I'll make it worth your while."

"I'll do that gladly Mr.."

"Chuds, just Chuds."

"Chuds you're gonna throw me out again aren't you?"

"Yes. Yes I am, how rough do you want it?"

"Full tilt Chuds, make it look real."

Chuds grabbed his arm and twisted it up behind his back before marching the huge man to the door, then opening it onto the street he pushed him roughly into the roadway. The big guy fell forward and didn't try to save himself at all. Laying on his front he received a forceful kick in the ribs and Chuds yelled, "Stay away from my friends!"

He walked over to Ro and said calmly, "Come on, let's go home."

She took his arm again and asked him what the hell had just happened.

"I think I just hired another security man."

Back at the apartment, they relaxed as best they could. Ro tried watching some TV but couldn't settle, so she went back to the balcony, Chuds grabbed a bottle of wine and two glasses and joined her.

Mostly they watched the river but sometimes Ro would bring up something about the Shisha Lounge, or tell an old story about her Mum which Chuds would counter with stories of his own. After a fairly long, but not uncomfortable silence RO turned to Chuds and asked him if he and Mona had ever had sex.

"Not once Ro, but she offered it many times."

"Yeah she told me that, I'm glad you didn't though."

"Why's that Ro?"

"'Cause I'm gonna fuck your brains out tonight Chuds Douglas, and I'm not sure whether it would have been awkward if I'd known that you'd done my Mum too."

"Ro, you don't have to do ..."

"Shut the fuck up, I'm not going to charge you."

Chapter 37

The next morning, when Chuds woke up she was gone again. He dressed and went to the kitchen where she was making toast and brewing coffee, she was wearing one of his t-shirts and seemingly little else.

"How did I do last night Chuds? Any brains left?"

"Some Ro but I'm pretty sure they're scrambled."

"Then my work is done," and she did a little curtsey.

"Chuds, I want to work on marketing stuff this morning and then we'll go see your legal eagle this afternoon. Does that work for you?"

"Sounds good Ro, I've got a meeting this morning here with the two guys from the e-arena module. They're bringing a cheque for their buy-in and we'll discuss the branding options and layout for the arena. I can meet them out here while you use the office."

He showered, dressed and washed the breakfast things while Ro went back into the office to work. His guests arrived at 10:00 and Chuds was surprised to see a young man and a young woman at the door. He ushered them in and put out a hand to the girl first, "Chuds, Chuds Douglas."

"I'm Plaid and this is Tommy, we're your tenants for the arena."

"I am truly sorry I had thought I was meeting two guys."

"Common mistake Chuds. There is no gender advantage to being an e-athlete. We compete on a level playing field, and I don't want to blow our own trumpets too much, but we are two of the best."

"Now **that** I had heard. Take a seat at the table let's get cracking." Chuds walked them through the contract and Plaid gave him the cheque. With contracts signed and exchanged they started to talk about the layout. The two gamers were very casual about the layout, just wanting to be the centre of attention on tournament nights, but were insistent on the equipment that they wanted installed. Between them they listed out everything and Chuds promised to get it to Deepa and keep them in the loop regarding installation.

Just then Ro walked out of the office, still wearing Chuds' T-Shirt and little else. She walked over to the table and Chuds introduced their guests. Ro shook hands with them both but seemed to hold Plaid's hand a little too long as she said, "Mm cute."

"Yeah I am ain't I?" and Plaid laughed.

"I want to go through the online marketing with you two and the branding, you up for a few more minutes?"

"Sure."

So Chuds stood and went back to the office to make some calls while the three of them started talking about social presence and in particular Twitch. When they had finished Ro called Chuds back in and they all shook hands before Plaid and Tommy left.

"They're nice," Ro commented.

"Ro, fancy lunch in town before we go to Anil's office?"

"You buying?"

"Sure."

"Then I'm eating. Should I get dressed?"

"Probably."

As they walked up the High Street, trying to decide where to have lunch they passed by Giovanni's, and Steve came running to the door to get their attention. He called them inside and shook Chuds' hand, who in turn introduced Ro.

"Oh yes, so sorry to hear about your Mother. Chuds we miss you here, I hope there's no hard feelings about me asking you to leave."

"None at all Steve, is everything okay here?"

"You have time for lunch? I can tell you what's been happening."

Steve showed them to a table and called a waitress to set three places for lunch, as they sat Steve started to explain how Johnny and Marti had rocked the restaurant on the evening that she had joined him for his second set. Apparently they had a natural chemistry and Steve described her voice as phenomenal! Many drinks were sent their way by happy customers and he had been getting calls asking when the two of them would be performing again.

She had apparently dropped a lot of hints about a new venue opening soon for karaoke and vocal coaching as well as parties and performances, there was a lot of interest.

"She's a treasure Chuds and she works so well with Johnny. Maybe we can do something with you when you open, kind of a joint promotion?"

"Anything is possible Steve, we'll talk about that. I'm so happy to hear it all went well. How's everything else?"

"As much as Johnny and Miss Marti brought customers in, Basha is driving them away. He brings girls in here that are so young you think they shouldn't be out that late at night. Then some creep will come in, join him at the table for a drink and leave with the girl. They look miserable and so young Chuds. I'm getting a bad reputation here. I asked him not to do it any more and he told me I had no choice, if I made trouble he'd burn the place to the ground."

Ro reached under the table and squeezed Chuds' thigh hard. He took her hand and held it tight and asked Steve to bear with the situation for a couple more weeks.

"I think something's going to happen soon Steve that'll make this problem go away for you."

Their food arrived and they all chatted and ate. When Chuds went to settle the bill, Steve told him it was on the house, they thanked him profusely and said they had a meeting to get to and left the restaurant, but not before Chuds went back into the kitchen to say hi to the staff. With a light rain beginning to fall they asked Steve to call a taxi and left by the back door to meet it in the car park.

The cab took them to Anil's offices and they were shown up to a small conference room where they sat at a long table and waited. Anil came in with a broad smile and a folder of papers, but as he looked at Ro he said quietly, "How are you doing?"

She shrugged and he sat at the table with them, opening the folder.

"Ro, your Mum left a kind of a will. Basically a set of instructions on what she wished to happen after her death and a short list of business interests, properties and cash accounts that should go to her sole heir, which would be you."

"It should also be noted that she had a joint business venture with Pete, she was in fact a partner not an employee. We'll cover the assets in a moment Ro. Is it okay if I talk about her wishes regarding her passing?"

"That's what we're here for right?"

"Fair enough Ro, I'm just trying to be a little sensitive here. Her primary wish for her remains was to be cremated."

"Job half done I'd say," Ro said somberly, "Maybe we can get a discount from the crematorium."

The room fell silent, nobody was quite sure what to say, until Chuds said, "For the best Ro, I didn't fancy being a pall bearer for your Mum's King Size Coffin."

She turned to him and punched his shoulder quite hard.

"Fuck you Chuds, your joke was better than mine. Anil, you obviously didn't know my Mum too well, I only made that joke because she would have said it if she was still here. Lighten up."

Anil coughed and attempted a smile, "Fair enough Ro, in my culture we don't.."

"Your culture?" Ro interrupted, "You're a GravesIndian Anil. Keep up!"

Anil placed the papers back on the table and looked over at Chuds, who grinned broadly. Ro snapped her fingers and said, "Oy Indian Colonel Sanders, look at me, it's my Mum we're talking about. Anil, I wasn't that close with my Mum but I did know her well, and for the record I hate knowing that I won't see her again. She was not a religious woman and actually the exact opposite of that. She hated fancy funerals calling them a waste of money so here's what I would like to happen."

Ro shuffled in her seat, took Chuds' hand and continued, "Send what's left of her to the crematorium and have them finish the job properly. Have them stick the ashes in a nice urn and keep them there until we open her Shisha lounge, then I'll pick them up. There's to be no service, no fancy ceremony, turn her to ash and hang on to her for a while."

Looking at Chuds she carried on, "The opening night of Sheikha's Shisha will be her celebration of life, it will be what she wanted the lounge to look like with one exception, there'll be a huge picture of Fat Mona, her urn and more alcohol than you can imagine. We will drink to her, to her life and to her dream realized and, Chuds Douglas, if it all goes well I may take you to one of the VIP rooms and do to you what I did last night."

Looking at Anil, Chuds said, "Got that?"

"I believe I do, Ro, you'll get what you want, you can count on it."

He picked up the paperwork again and shuffled some papers to the front of the pile.

"Now to your Mum's assets Ro. You are declared as her only next of kin and all assets and legal entities pass to you. Your Mum had three freehold houses currently being rented out and making a satisfactory income, at the last tax assessment these properties were valued at 2.6 million."

Ro looked up quickly, "Pounds?"

"Yes, 2.6 million pounds Ro, she had two interest bearing accounts with a current worth of 480,000 and, before you ask, yes pounds. She was also a partner in two businesses with Pete including the pub. You own 50% of those. There will be quite a bit of tax but I have a good man who can limit your exposure on there. Your gross worth is approaching 4 million pounds and if you give me the go ahead I'll have my guy work out a way to pay as little tax as possible on that."

Ro looked at Chuds, her expression was one of complete shock, she gave him a questioning look with her eyes and he nodded that, in his opinion, she should give the go ahead.

"Go ahead Anil, set your man loose."

Chapter 38

The next few days were spent on the building project. Ro had decided to stay at the apartment for a while, reminding Chuds on several occasions that he had said she could stay as long as she wanted to.

"And I meant it," was always his reply.

She worked on the online presence, asking Chuds for his opinions on design elements for the website, and building a social media presence for the group and the individual modules. She was good, very good and she also spent a lot of time and energy drawing out plans for the Shisha Lounge and researching décor and furniture. She had ordered a considerable number of Hookah sets and was also busy recruiting girls to act as hosts. After a few days of work, over lunch one day, she looked at Chuds and he met her gaze evenly.

"Chuds, in case you hadn't noticed, I've come off the game."

"I wasn't sure if you had Ro, or if you were just taking a rest."

"No, I retired Chuds, just as well or your account would be huge by now," and she winked, "I wanna concentrate on the lounge and the business Chuds. I'm management now."

"And very good at it Ro, congratulations."

As they finished their lunch Chuds took the dishes to the sink and started to wash them. The doorbell chimed and Ro went to the intercom. She came back to announce that there was a Francois Trouver at the door for him, "Funny thing though Chuds, Monsieur Trouver sounds like he's from Birmingham not Calais."

"Send him through Ro, our security manager is here."

Greg Wallace climbed the steps up to the apartment and was greeted by Ro, who ushered him in.

"Wild Man!" Chuds walked quickly to the door to shake the hand of the new visitor, Ro looked him up and down and said quietly, "Fuck me, you don't get many of those to the pound."

Chuds made the introductions, gave a very brief account of having worked with Greg in Africa and explained how a Legionnaire could get French nationality after completing a minimum of five years service.

"Hence, Monsieur Trouver with a Brummie accent."

Chuds made some coffee and they sat at the dining table. He gave Francois a fairly thorough briefing on what had happened and what would be expected of him.

"You know my work ethic Chuds, you'll get the best from me."

"I know it Greg, wait you still answer to Greg?"

"I'll answer to pretty much anything Chuds, and I have a report for you from Marvin."

"Okay, let's hear what you've got."

Reaching into a messenger bag, Greg pulled out a large folder and opened it to the front page.

"I've read through this Chuds, I hope we can clear this slimebag out of your town. You wanna read this or shall I summarize?"

"You tell us both what you got Greg, damn it is SO good to see you."

Greg started to summarize the results of Marvin's investigation, it seems that Basha had originally entered the country on a travel permit as Albania was not a member of the Schengen Accord and had simply stayed. His wife, although ethnically Albanian was a British Citizen, and she and several relatives all started sponsoring visitor visas for cousins and nieces.

Forged ID documents at their country of origin became linked to the biometrics taken to obtain the visas so the girls more or less passed through immigration unchecked. However, the sheer number of visas applied for had aroused suspicion and put flags on fresh arrivals but nothing had ever been shown or proven to be false.

The girls never overstayed their visas and frequently left the country before the expiry date, which further lessened the urgency to investigate them as they were obviously not trying to stay illegally. Now the NCA was investigating Basha though as some of the girls had been arrested in Thailand and saved from a trafficking ring. The names they gave did not match their documentation and they told of being sold as sex workers to bar owners and pimps.

When that investigation, which revealed that they had changed their travel plans in Mainland Europe and instead of returning to Albania they had travelled on to Asia, bumped into the Immigration investigation suspicions were aroused across the board. However, it was relatively low level and was sitting on a desk somewhere waiting for action.

Marvin had used some high level contacts and if they could get conclusive evidence, preferably while a crime was actually being committed, the NCA and Immigration were prepared to mainline the case.

Chuds picked up his phone and called Brian.

"Bri, have you got a list of all the spa properties that we lost to the Basha crew?"

"I can get it Chuds, why?"

"I'll explain later Bri. Get the list together and send it to Ro on her email."

Looking at Greg he said, "I have a plan developing in my mind. We used to run a few spas in the area but lost all the leases. I would bet they are now scruffy knocking shops and prisons for these poor girls. Also if we could find out when the next girls are due to arrive we could get Marvin's contacts in the NCA and Immigration to flag the arrival and interview the girls and whoever is meeting them at Heathrow. We could coordinate raids on the properties with the girls being held at the airport and I think I also have a way to get some dirt on Basha, but it might put you in harms way Greg."

"Fucking hell Chuds, I lived in harms way for over 10 years, sign me up boss."

Chapter 39

The next 2 weeks were a busy combination of business planning and of virtual meetings with Marvin and Greg to formulate a plan to take down Basha. Chuds and Ro met with Johnny and Marti to discuss the full layout and equipment needs of the karaoke centre. Marti and Ro hit it off immediately, and the ideas flowed for the branding, décor and layout quickly.

Meetings followed with Deepa and Brian to arrange the fit-out of the interior and planning applications were rushed through by Anil to get full construction under way as quickly as possible. Brian also coordinated hiring with Chuds to get staff for all the venues, and Pete, now out of hospital and without the burden of the pub, started planning the catering and bar dispensary.

Simultaneously Chuds was talking with Marvin and Greg regarding the security for the building and the plan to deal with Basha. Chuds sent the list of properties that they had lost over to Marvin and he had men and women observing them, noting who went in and out and trying to find out who was living there.

Finally they got advice that two of Basha's 'nieces' would be arriving at Heathrow, travelling alone and would have to be met by a relative at the arrival gate. Marvin coordinated with immigration and arranged to have them detained and questioned on arrival and the 'family member' that would be meeting them detained separately and interrogated.

The final piece of this puzzle for Chuds was to get Basha to incriminate himself also. He called Steve at the restaurant to see if he would arrange a meeting with Basha, timed to coincide with the arrivals at Heathrow and the raids at the properties.

Steve sounded understandably nervous, but Chuds assured him that it would end his problem, he encouraged him to ask Basha to the restaurant to plead with him to stop bringing the girls in there.

"The timing has to be right though Steve, you have to get him there on the date and time that I send you."

"If you're sure Chuds, I trust you but I don't want trouble in the restaurant."

"I can't promise that won't happen Steve, but I'll keep it as low key as I can."
When he finished the conversation with Steve, Ro looked at him and, in a calm voice, told him, "When you go for that prick, I want to be there Chuds."

"It could get a bit hairy Ro, you sure you're up for it?"

"You couldn't stop me if you tried."

"Fair enough, I may even have a job for you."

He contacted Marvin to arrange to borrow a couple of wire surveillance sets which arrived the next day and then he contacted Steve again to arrange the meeting for next evening at 7:00 pm.

Chuds went over the plan with Greg and Ro, there would have to be safety parameters set in and alternate courses of action depending on events, but at 6:30 the following night Chuds fitted Ro with a mic and recorder concealed beneath her clothes and put one on himself also.

Then they set out to walk up the High Street and appear to be passing Giovanni's.

The three of them, Chuds, Ro and Greg got to the window of the restaurant and saw Basha and Steve at the table, arguing. Behind Basha stood the big guy that had approached Chuds for work, arms crossed looking disinterested.

They entered the restaurant and approached the table. Basha saw them and ushered Steve away, then indicated to his bodyguard to search Greg and Chuds. They both put their arms out and he frisked Greg, finding nothing and then went to Chuds. He pulled the recorder from Chuds' chest and yanked the mic away too, throwing both pieces on the table.

Basha looked at them and smiled, "Really? A set up and you thought I wouldn't check? Sit Mr Douglas, sit."

"What? You don't call me Chuds any more?"

"I think those days ended when you started attacking my men."

"To be fair I only did that to protect some poor girl independent contractors."

"Who were infringing on MY business Mr. Douglas."

"I think they were all a little old for your business Basha."

Basha smirked but remained seated at the table. "Still I had hoped that we wouldn't have to fight Mr. Douglas but it seems you left me no choice."

"Mr. Basha I only wanted to open an entertainment complex and renovate a building that means a lot to me for sentimental reasons."

"Ah, but I heard about your VIP rooms and what that fat cow was planning to do there. I had to stop that, and I may do to your new project what I had done to that pub that she ran with the old queer."

Chuds felt Ro bristle, she stood to his left about one step behind him, but he could feel her tense when Basha mentioned the pub and her Mum.

He hoped she would stay cool.

"Mr Basha, I hate to tell you this but I think that your business days are numbered in this town. Actually I don't hate to tell you that at all. It makes me very happy to think that my town, the town that I was born and raised in, will be rid of scum like you."

"Ah, your town? You used to be a King here didn't you? What are you going to do Mr. Douglas, you think your big man will protect you from me and my big man?"

Chuds looked at Greg and gave him a wink.

"Oh he's not here to protect me, he's here to hold me back if things get out of control."

Basha laughed out loud, "You? You think you can do anything to me?"

Chuds made an exaggerated look at his watch, "Well Mr Basha, not only me. In exactly..." he glanced at his watch again, "seven minutes, the NCA, Home Office Investigators and members of the Kent Police force will simultaneously raid every property that you took from my old company. They have been watching them for days now and all occupants will be taken for questioning and vetting regarding their true identities in conjunction with Interpol. At the same time the two 'nieces' arriving at Heathrow aboard Air Albania Flight 0667 will be taken to a secure office for exhaustive questioning to establish the validity of their visas and the family member of yours that was going to meet them will, instead, meet immigration and law enforcement officers in their own interrogation room. Am I making this scenario clear enough for you?"

Basha reached for his phone but Greg pinned his arm to the table. Basha, for the first time began to look worried and turned to look at his bodyguard who appeared to be busy looking at his phone. As his head turned back to look at Chuds he was just in time to see Ro pull an 8 inch Ka-Bar knife from her bag and hand it, handle first, to Chuds, who flipped it blade down and immediately slammed it down hard into the back of Basha's hand. He felt it hit, pass through the hand and the tip just slightly enter the table top.

Basha's jaw dropped and he let out a scream, turning his head he yelled at his bodyguard, "Help you lazy cunt!"

"Sure thing boss," and he put his huge hand onto the knife handle and pressed it down hard, completely pinning Basha's hand to the table while looking at Chuds and smiling.

Chuds called out, "Bring them in Steve."

Eight armed police officers entered the dining area and Chuds pulled the knife from Basha's Hand and gave it to Greg, who immediately bolted from the restaurant and ran down to the riverfront where he heaved the knife into the Thames. The police pulled Basha roughly to his feet and cuffed him. He yelled out with pain as his sliced hand was pinned behind his back and screamed obscenities at Chuds and Ro and about Chuds and Ro.

"Oh, that hurts," Ro looked at Chuds and mouthed, "Thank you."

Chuds stood and walked to the Police Sergeant, "Do you need us for anything?"

"I don't believe so Sir, we can take a full statement later but the restaurant owner says Basha tried to attack you and you defended yourself with," he looked at his notebook, "a steak knife. From the look of that wound it was a fucking big steak knife... Sir."

Chuds shrugged, "That's exactly how it went, hey hold on a minute Sergeant," Chuds reached his hand up under Ro's shirt.

"Hoy! Money up front Sailor," and she giggled. Chuds pulled the recorder from her stomach and removed the SD Card which he handed to the cop.

"You might find the contents of this interesting," then looking at Ro he said, "Hey Francois is outside, shall we go for dinner now? Fancy a Chinese?"

"Don't know, is he a good looking Chinese?"

"Of course, think I'd fix you up with a minger?"

The police Sergeant yelled after them, "Sir, Sir what happened to the Steak Knife?"

"I think the dishwasher took it."

As they were leaving the restaurant, Basha's bodyguard, who was talking to a police constable looked over at Chuds who said to him, "You're hired by the way, report tomorrow morning at 10:00 am."

"Report where Boss?"

"Figure that out yourself or you're fired."

Chapter 40

The next morning Chuds called Steve and asked if everything was okay at the restaurant. He even offered to pay for the table that he had damaged with the knife. Steve told him that the table was staying exactly as it was, and now belonged to Chuds, any time he wanted a reservation that was his table for life.

"I appreciate that Steve, I hope we didn't damage your reputation there too much."

"If anything you enhanced it Chuds, come for dinner soon and bring that gorgeous girl with you."

Chuds smiled at that, people assumed they were a couple now. Were they?

He called Marvin for a progress report on the raids and the airport. Nine young girls aged from 11 to 14 were in local care and being counselled, they were scared, yet relieved and were cooperating fully with the police and social workers. The girls at the airport were also being counselled and were telling everything about their kidnapping in Albania, threats made regarding their parents if they didn't cooperate with authorities and how scared they were at being sent to a new country alone. The family member meeting the girls was a sister-in-law of Basha and was currently in custody.

"And Basha?"

"Basha will be charged in a few days, the police are preparing charges of conspiracy to kidnap, human trafficking, conspiracy to provide Class A drugs and overstaying a travel permit. Also as accelerant had been found at the scene of the fire a charge of conspiracy to commission a murder was added."

"It's gonna take months to try him Chuds, but the good news is he'll be in custody until his trial and they don't like nonce's much in prison. It's possible he won't even last until his trial. In fact I can put a word in and make sure he doesn't if you say the word."

"I'd never do that Marvin, his welfare is none of my concern, just don't let them set the fucker free."

"No chance of that happening Chuds."

He made coffee, pulled Ro from the bed and dragged her out to the balcony where she sat on his lap while they both sipped from their mugs.

Chapter 41

The next three months were a steady stream of planning meetings, recruitment drives and equipment purchases.

Money started to come on from the grant applications and the interior of the Regal Entertainment complex really began to take shape. The exterior was renovated to its former glory as it looked when it was a major cinema in the old town.

Ro's inheritance was settled and she was now a wealthy young lady. The question as to whether they were a couple remained unanswered, but she was living at the apartment and evidentially it would appear that they were. He had no complaints.

Basha was officially charged with a laundry list of offences and a trial date set. However, he didn't make the trial as he was stabbed to death by a lifer who apparently didn't like child abusers. Nobody in Chuds' circle of friends wept for him, or even cared really.

The closer it got to the building being completed, Ro started developing plans for a series of 'Invite Only' soft opening events. Each module would hold its own premiere evening, starting with the e-Arena. Plaid and Tommy would attempt to break a world record for a game called Mobile Legends.

"It's a bit old school Chuds," Plaid had told him, "but it is actually an event in the South East Asian Games and in other major international events, we'll bring in a couple of special guests and we'll get gaming companies to sponsor us with give-aways and prizes."

Chuds had organized a showing of "One Flew Over the Cuckoo's Nest" for the cinema's premiere, which would be the second event and the publisher's of Ken Kesey's book were going to provide a bunch of free copies. The opening evening would include a free dinner and wine served while watching the movie.

The following night Sovereign's Song Palace would open with a grand catered party, karaoke competitions and a performance by Marti and Johnny, with the promise of special guest vocalists. Steve was already pushing the event at Giovanni's and had promised to close the restaurant on the opening night and bring all of the staff. Johnny and Marti were performing there every weekend to sold out crowds and pushing the venue as well.

The last of the opening events would be Sheikha's Shisha Lounge and Ro was handling this one all by herself, coordinating only with Deepa, who had put herself through law school by working for Fat Mona. She had licensed a complete library of modern oriental beats based music by some of the world's best. She designed and ordered tailored uniforms for the girls with an eastern theme, yet tastefully erotic, and all of the girls had been trained in hookah management and hygiene.

As the date drew closer Ro ramped up the social media marketing and a countdown timer appeared on the website. There was a buzz in the town and both Chuds and Ro did interviews on local radio and there was even an appearance on National morning television.

Finally the opening week arrived, all four events were sold out and walk-throughs and rehearsals had been held at every venue the week before. Nerves were running high but there was an underpinning of confidence and excitement.

The Mobile Legends event was a major success with Plaid setting a new high score record, the event streamed live on Twitch and already major publishers and sponsors were approaching them to offer sponsorship deals.

The movie night was fully attended, Pete provided an amazing set menu dinner with champage, the publishing company sent three boxes of Ken Kesey's book and United Artists sent posters, prop replicas and autographed photos.

Johnny and Marti's Karaoke opener was completely booked out, with tickets being bought and sold locally during the week prior. The entire staff of Giovanni's showed up and Steve even brought the table complete with the knife mark where Basha's hand had been pinned to it. The man who liked to be called Antonio sang a song, "froma the olda country" to which the crowd roared "Where's that? Dartford?"

There were also guest appearances from three major recording artists that Marti had sung with and karaoke competitions with prizes that included concert tickets and compact discs.

Then it was the turn of Sheikha's Shisha Lounge. The customer base was about 70% male and 30% couples. The guests walked past a life size photo board of Fat Mona and her urn was discretely placed behind the display. There were tables and booths with plush furnishings and the waitress staff looked incredible in the uniforms designed by Ro.

Orders were taken for Shisha flavours, hookah's brought in, glowing charcoal installed and complimentary hummus, pita bread and snacks provided free of charge. Anil, Deepa and some of the legal staff took up two tables and Chuds and Ro sat with them.

In truth Ro did not do much sitting, she fluttered around like a butterfly, talking to customers, assisting the girls, helping Pete deliver the champagne and checking with the security staff, headed up by Basha's Big Guy, who had been assigned to the Shisha business permanently.

About 2 hours into the evening she grabbed Chuds' hand and said, "Come with me."

No VIP rooms were being used on the opening night, but she quickly unlocked one, pulled Chuds inside then locked the door behind them. Throwing her arms around his neck she kissed him passionately, "Mum would love this, thank you for making this happen" she said, then as she pushed him down onto the majilis cushioning, "She might even have liked this bit."

The four events were a resounding success. Online reviews were incredibly positive and the website membership and event booking forms were filling up.

On the first fully operational night, with all modules open to the public, the venue was buzzing with excitement. Marvin was there and, wanting to relive his glory days as the singer with Red Amber and the Green Lights, had to be pulled away from the mic to give other customers a chance. Even with the words on the screen he couldn't get them right but he could still carry a tune.

The cinema was showing a remastered copy of Casablanca and

membership surveys were being distributed to get ideas for more classic movies to be shown.

Chuds checked in with security, under the watchful eye of Francois Trouver, before going downstairs to the basement area where had an office. He opened the door and entered the plush interior. The seating was all covered in velvet like the old cinema seats had been. Steve had donated the actual table that Basha's hand had been impaled on and there was a large desk that was modelled on an old Cinema kiosk using wood salvaged from the old cinema.

On one wall hung a beautiful picture of his Grandparents, digitally enhanced and beautifully printed on canvas. Sitting at his desk he remembered coming to the cinema as a very young boy with his Grandad to see Ben Hur, and he imagined his Grandfather there now holding his hand. Two large monitor screens showed the output from the CCTV cameras and watching the venue's interior, humming with activity, he smiled broadly.

He loved his new building, loved the direction his life was taking with Ro and he especially loved his new office.

An office that was fit for purpose.

Fit for a King.

Afterword

Absolutely none of this book is true, well, maybe some bits, but mostly it's a pack of lies inspired by real people and events.

I would especially like to offer thanks to a few people:

- My wife, Veronica, for letting me do this when I should have been washing the dishes.

- David John Griffin for always helping me out, beta reading the whole thing and pushing me through a writer's block.

- Terry Lee, the (incredibly handsome) landlord of the Red Lion for allowing me to use his pub in one of the stories and for being a true mate.

- My niece Mica who I bounced ideas off repeatedly while I was supposed to be helping her in our shop.

- Saad Chishty for providing the soundtrack that I wrote almost everything to.

Anyone who recognizes themselves in this work of fiction, if you like the character, it really is based on you, if you're offended, get a grip, it's obviously meant to be someone else.

And to anyone that takes the time to read this, thank you.

Check out Peter Draper's other books on Amazon, including...

The Timeliness Trilogy

This collection of three novellas follows the journey of Dr.Peter Castell, a military Physicist who develops a revolutionary technology that has the potential to change tactical and humanitarian protocols forever.

A compelling tale, the first part "Timeliness" covers the origins and progress of a Top Secret Military Project that is researching the possibility of using time and space adjustment in a tactical scenario. It follows the life and work of Castell as he leads his team through months of research and encounters moments of triumph, failure and danger as he, and his team, turn their hypotheses into a viable program.

The Second book follows this narrative as the Project develops and actually undertakes their first tactical mission using their new technology. The book explores the dilemma of paradox and looks at the horrible choices that the team has to face along the way. It explores how good and bad deeds are sometimes interchangeable and how the significance of events can almost never be predicted.

Part three "Revolution and Resolution" sees a major character try and manipulate the project's technology for truly horrendous purposes, and the team's response to the threat of their mission being derailed. How far are they willing to let this man go before something has to be done, and what will be the repercussions?

Available in Paperback, Hardback and Kindle e-book from Amazon

Printed in Great Britain
by Amazon